CRIMSON HEIR

"What was that about? That vampire is still alive!" Jim
shouted.

"Calm down." Vic's hands patted the air trying to calm
Jim from a distance. "We are going to kill her."

"To live like that. Even a second." Jim shook with
repressed anger. "It's wrong."

"I know. I know." Vic looked Jim in the eye. "I know. I
understand. But this is bigger than anything else we've
ever done. This might be it. Just this once. We've got her
caged. It's not like she can hurt anyone."

Truck and Stevo said nothing, just stood behind Vic,
waiting to see if Jim would need any extra restraint.

Seething with fury, Jim said, "You wouldn't coddle me
like this. If I wanted to keep a vampire alive."

"You can't do what he does." Vic shrugged. "I've never
found anyone that can and will do what he does."

CRIMSON HEIR

By D.L. Lawson

ibooks

DISTRIBUTED BY PUBLISHERS GROUP WEST

An original ibooks, inc Book.

Copyright © 2005 ibooks, inc.

Distributed by Publishers Group West
1700 Fourth Street, Berkeley, California 94710
www.pgw.com

ibooks, inc.
24 West 25th Street
New York, NY 10010

ISBN: 1-59687-165-2
First Printing December 2005

Printing in the USA

Dedication
For all those bad girls out there who want to be
vampires, and for Miss Kimberly, the original

Acknowledgment
With special thanks to the music of Evanescence

CHAPTER ONE

Raven spotted the wanna-be about halfway through the first set. The moody low stage lighting enabled her to see the audience as well as it could see her. Being able to see the crowd was an old paranoia that she wouldn't let go. It had saved her life too many times in the past.

Raven moved so she and Clarisa sang on either side of the mic, their voices blending in a harmony that Raven had been told sent chills up spines. Her guitar and Clarisa's bass facing each other, bleeding into the pickups on the other instrument, adding to the eerie quality of the song.

When the song ended, Raven moved back to her own mic and began the next number. Again her eyes found the wanna-be in the crowd. She made eye contact with people in the swaying audience while she sang, but her eyes kept going back to the man her mind had labeled a wanna-be.

It wasn't so much his clothing that made him stand

out. Half the audience was in black T-shirts and jeans. There were always a few newbies in a Goth crowd, someone new to the lifestyle but those people were usually with someone, showing them the ropes. What made him stand out was the way he spent more time watching the crowd rather than the band. He reminded her of a farm boy on his first trip to the big city.

The song faded out except for Tina's drum solo. She made a smooth transition to a faster tempo. Clarisa added her bass to the mix, and a measure later Raven joined in. The arrangement had the desired effect, slowly pumping up the audience until they were jumping up and down in place. It was the Sinister Sisters' tribute to the punk sound and never failed to make the audience dance in place.

While she sang Raven watched the wanna-be. She was amused by his antics and expressions. At the moment he was practically staring open mouthed at a busty redhead in tight stretch pants and a lace corset. She must have noticed the farm boy watching her and decided to have some fun. The way she moved would have been enough to start wars in some countries, and she seemed to be directing her wiggles at the slack-jawed goof.

The next song was the last before they took a break. The idea was to give the audience a chance to catch their breath after the rowdiness of the previous song. Calm them down, play to their hearts and not their desire to be pumped up, and they were likely to stay for their second set rather than wonder off. The manager of the club only let them sell their CDs at the end of the show, so they wanted to keep everyone there.

The song was a moody piece about lost love and lost hope that was a fan favorite. The lyrics were simple and short, the strength of the song relying on the precision of the music and the blues-style guitar licks. The audience swayed and moved together as one, becoming a part of the show. Raven looked out to see if the wanna-be had taken the opportunity to get closer to the redhead, but he no where to be seen. *A bashful farm boy*, Raven thought as she hit the minor chord ending the song.

"Thank you," Raven said to a mostly quiet audience. Silence was the appropriate form of appreciation for that song. Applause of any kind would have broken the tableau that had been created between the band and the audience. They sensed it and no one broke it, allowing the emotion of the song to linger.

"We're going to take a short break, and then we'll be back to play for another hour," said Raven.

Putting a break into their show had been done on the insistence of the club manager, Charlie. The band could have played straight through, but the manager told them he didn't sell as many drinks when there was no break. It always sounded shady to Raven, but it wasn't something she had control over. So the band made a wardrobe change during their forced break.

Raven and the others were leaving the remodeled closet that was referred to as a dressing room. There was a commotion going on by the stage door and the three looked around the corner to see what was going on. Raven was shocked to see the wanna-be trying to force his way past Manny. Manny carried a solid two hundred fifty pounds on his 5'10" frame. The wanna-

3

be was being slowly eased out by Manny's bulk.

The wanna-be made eye contact with Raven, and his efforts redoubled.

"I have to see you," he shouted. "I want to talk to you."

"Buy a ticket like everyone else, kid," said Manny as he forced the door closed the final few inches.

"What was that all about?" Tina asked as they made their way back to the stage.

"I have no idea," said Raven. "I saw him in the audience during the first set, but he only had eyes for some redhead in the crowd. He was doing the swivel-headed wanna-be routine."

"It's amazing what a little cleavage will make a guy do," said Clarisa.

The three laughed as they stepped back onto the stage and picked up their instruments. The second set was arranged to be a more forceful, louder, and faster group of songs. For this set the Sinister Sisters wanted to get the crowd pumped. Have their hearts racing and the endorphins flowing, having a natural high kicking in with whatever they were drinking or whatever. And if a happy crowd bought a few more CDs, it paid the rent.

During the second song Raven spotted the wanna-be back in the audience. She was afraid for a minute that he would try to rush the stage to get at her. She tensed, ready to retreat back from the edge of the stage, or kick him back if need be. Raven watched, but he never made a move toward the stage. Not only that, but he wasn't watching the band. Raven followed his gaze across the room, expecting to find the busty redhead at the end of his stare.

Without an immediate threat to worry her, Raven was able to relax and get into the energy of the song. The smell of booze, cigarettes, and human sweat filled the air. Bopping up and down to the rhythm of the song, she moved around the stage and was able to get in a better position to see what farm boy was looking at. She was surprised to see not the busty redhead, but almost her polar opposite. Dancing in place where he was looking Raven saw only a waif-like Goth girl.

The girl looked barely legal. She had short black hair in a spiky style and wore a leather jacket over her T-shirt despite the heat of the room. She was rocking and dancing in place, watching the band and unaware she was being watched.

As the second set progressed, Raven kept track of where the wanna-be was in the room. She watched as he worked his way through the crowd to the Goth girl. Not knowing whether the girl was in danger from the wanna-be, Raven kept looking at her. While she was moving her fingers faster than most thought possible, working through a high-pitched piercing guitar solo, something that had been niggling in the back of her mind jumped forward and made Raven fumble the last couple of chords.

She was able to recover and was sure only Clarisa and Tina knew she had flubbed it. After getting back into the groove of the song, Raven took a closer look at the Goth girl. She was no kid in upscale black clothing. Raven was looking at another vampire, and one she didn't know.

Vampires had always mixed well with the Goth culture. Raven was familiar with the vampires in Los

Angeles that frequented the club scene. The sleep-all-day, party-all-night approach to life appealed to many of those who couldn't go out in the sun. She wasn't sure if any of them knew she was also a vampire. Raven worked hard to appear human.

Raven took care in how she spoke and where the mic was when she sang so her fangs were not very noticeable. The few people that had noticed and asked, she told them a story about cosmetic dentistry in Miami. Other than staying out of the sun, Raven tried to follow very human habits. She had even gotten to where she could eat at a restaurant with her human friends, albeit very rare burgers. And when she was driven by hunger to feed, well, LA was full of homeless people who, sadly but thankfully, weren't missed when she was done.

But this vampire was unknown to her. She didn't carry herself as one recently converted either. Raven wondered where she came from. Why was she here in this club? Was she looking for Raven?

Raven gave a three count that launched into a Nirvana cover. She tried to focus on her performance, but the night was throwing too many oddities at her. First the wanna-be trying to crash the back door during intermission. Now there was an unknown vampire in the audience that has the wanna-be's attention. Were they working together? From a locked door in her mind a fear Raven tried to keep back started to break out. Was Demetri still looking for her?

Raven feared Demetri more than vampire hunters. She felt a shudder run down her back. She tried to focus on the music and push Demetri out of her mind. It had been too long and she was afraid where that fear might lead.

Raven finished the song and while she caught her breath she scanned the crowd closer. She had allowed herself to get lax in her precautions. A few years ago she would never have allowed herself to stand in front of hundreds of strangers like this. But an eternal life cringing in fear was no life at all. Slowly she had allowed herself to join the rest of the world. When she met Clarisa and Tina and they accepted her as a normal, she allowed herself to hope she could integrate with their lives and remain hidden.

The last song was one Tina had written ten minutes after being dumped by a jerk of a boyfriend. The venom of the lyrics was filled with emotion and images of that relationship. Raven hadn't let Tina make any changes after she had calmed down a couple days later. There was power in the words used at the height of emotion. Their audiences agreed and now they used it to close their show.

Raven looked into the crowd. She found her vampire waif still in the same spot, moving with the crowd to the beat of the drum. It looked to Raven like she was just enjoying the show like everyone else in the room. Looking around she couldn't see the psychopathic farm boy wanna-be. She squinted and tried to peer deeper into the back of the room, but still couldn't locate her quarry.

Raven hit the final power chord and let it fade into the room. "Thank you, we are the Sinister Sisters."

This time the room was filled with applause, shouts, and whistles. Normally Raven got a rush at the end of the show. The band and the audience were breathing hard, almost in unison, sweat glistening on skin. There was something exhilarating and draining at the same time. Clarisa always said it was as close to sex as you can get without touching.

The applause died down and the crowd moved back toward the bar for more drinks. The band may be done, but the party was still going.

"You doing okay, sweetie? You seemed to be having some dizzy spells or something."

Raven turned to Clarisa. "Sorry. I'm not sure what happened. Maybe I got some bad sushi."

Tina snorted as she came around from behind her drums. "Yeah, right. More likely it's one of those burgers you like to eat cooked so rare I can swear they are mooing. I keep telling you, come over to the dark side. Be a vegan like me. And look at the killer bod that comes with it," Tina said as she raised her arms above her head and did a slow spin.

"I've met your mother, Tina, and I would say a good part of that killer bod comes from good genetics," Raven said as she poked Tina's exposed stomach.

Raven moved to the side of the stage and put her guitar into its case. "I'm okay. Sorry about my finger stumbles, but that guy that was yelling at us during the break was back in the audience during the second set. I was worried he'd do something stupid."

"Yeah, I saw him, too," said Clarisa. "I was ready to give him a spike in the face if he tried to jump on the stage."

Clarisa kicked the air in front of her as if she were aiming her boot heel at a target. Raven and Tina laughed with her.

The three were able to break down the drums and store them in their cases with a speed that came from lots of practice. Raven kept looking into the crowd to see if the wanna-be had come back. He hadn't, and now the new vampire was no where to be seen either.

The dressing room was turned back into a closet when they stored their instruments until the next night. At least they were under lock and key so no one would mess with them. They had tried to leave the stage set between shows, but there was always someone at the bar who thought they could have been a rock star if they'd just gotten that big break. The number of broken strings alone had made the daily breakdown and set up worth the time.

Normally the three of them would go out to the greasy spoon around the corner for something to eat. Raven's old fears had been pushed into her face and until she knew what was going on she didn't want to put her friends in danger. She knew she could hold her own against another vampire, but if Clarisa and Tina were with her, they could be hurt and they didn't heal as fast as she did.

As they started to leave the stage area Raven stopped. "I forgot some music I was working on in the dressing room. You guys go on and I'll catch up."

"Want some help?" Clarisa asked.

"No, I know where it is. I'll just have to move a few drum boxes to get to it. You guys go eat. I'll meet up with you later," Raven said while waving them toward the door.

Raven moved behind the stage. She planned to climb to the roof and take a birds-eye-view of the neighborhood. She may have allowed her caution to wane, but she was going to make sure she found out what was going on.

At the far corner of the backstage area there was a ladder mounted into the wall. Which lead to a hatch cover that opened to the roof. When Raven put her hand on the rung she thought she heard a noise behind her.

"Manny?" Raven called out as she turned her head. There was no response.

Raven turned toward Manny's backstage station, the place he sat and read his books while the show was going on. His job was to keep peace backstage. Some of the acts could get out of hand. Usually he went out front after the show was over.

She heard the sound again and Raven paused in her approach to where he would be. "Manny?" she called louder.

Realizing she was shouting her position to someone who might be stalking her, say some unknown vampire or her accomplice, Raven moved into a shadows against the back wall, her clothing helping her to blend in and her black Converse making her movement silent. She cocked her ear toward where she had last heard the sound.

She couldn't hear anything except the muffled sounds of the people partying out front. No fluttering curtains, no shoe scrapes, no heavy breathing. But there was a hint of cologne. The problem was Raven didn't know if it was Manny's or not. She was going to have to go into hunt-and-search mode.

Crouching down, Raven began to move along the

back wall. Having been playing regularly at this club she knew the backstage area well. She knew where the piles of crap being saved for some future use where stacked and how to avoid them.

Raven shifted to move around a stack of scaffolding materials when she felt someone grab her belt in the middle of her back. Just as quick she was being jerked backwards and up.

She started to lose her balance as she was pulled back, and rather than fight it she let her body go with the roll. Whoever had been pulling her was forced to let go instead of falling with her. Raven fell toward the stage, tucking into a roll to absorb the fall. She came up with fangs bared and her fingers extended into claws. She was about to launch herself at her attacker in the shadows when she heard someone chuckling from that direction.

"Whoa, darlin'. You could hurt someone with those," said the tall lanky vampire that stepped out of the shadows. He was dressed much like Raven, black jeans and shirt, but he was wearing a pair of pointy-toed, black, cowboy boots. His dark hair was slicked back behind his ears.

"Cowboy?" Raven shouted as she dropped her defenses and leapt into his arms. She kissed him deep, holding his head in her hands. When she released him, he seemed in a daze. Until she slapped him across the face.

"Ouch! What was that for?" said Cowboy as he rubbed his jaw.

"For scaring the shit out of me," said Raven. "I haven't seen you for six years and this is how you greet me? What the hell were you doing back here?"

Raven had straightened her clothes from her tumble, but she continued to glare at Cowboy.

"Well, I could tell you I was just having some fun with you, like the old days," said Cowboy. He tried to give her an ah-shucks look but Raven wasn't letting it go. "Or I could tell you I was testing you to see if you were on your toes."

"I guess you got your answer. I was about to kick your ass," said Raven finally releasing him from her glare as she leaned in to hug him again.

Cowboy returned the embrace, then turned her so they were walking with arms around each other. "Darlin' I hate to break it to you, but there were at least three times when I could have taken you out with a crossbow bolt."

"It's been tried before, and I'm still here," said Raven.

"True. Listen, is there someplace we can talk?" asked Cowboy.

Raven smiled at him. "We could go to my place, but I'd be afraid the big bad cowboy would steal this little native princess's land."

Raven felt Cowboy's hand slide off her shoulder and slap her butt. "Just a chance you're going to have to take," he said.

A few minutes later Raven was in the passenger seat of a new Mazda. "It's a rental," Cowboy said. "I still haven't given up on pickup trucks yet, despite the price of gas."

"So what have you been doing lately," Raven asked after she'd given him directions to her apartment.

"Building amusement parks for vampires," said Cowboy.

"Fine, don't tell me," said Raven.

"No, I'm serious. I hit on this idea and it's taken off. Oh, they're not really parks *per se*, more like fantasy rooms."

"Okay, now I'm curious, tell me more," she said.

"About four years ago, I set up a construction company to bring in some money. You know how it is, even vampires have to pay the rent. I cater to our kind. A lot of vampires want to have work done on their places, but it's hard to trust normals. You never know when one is going to have ties with a hunter. By using me they know they're okay. I hire some of the other vampires, and even have a normal crew for anything that has to be done in the daylight."

"That sounds like a great idea," said Raven, "but where do the fantasy rooms come in?"

Cowboy finished making a left hand turn before answering. "Well, one ol' boy had me build him a panic room. Deep in his basement away from any light sources and such. A place he could bolt if some hunters broke in on him. It wasn't a very big space, maybe six foot across. The thing is this guy doesn't want to get bored while he's hiding, so he has a big screen television installed along one wall."

"You're kidding."

"Nope. But that's what gave me the idea. I used the designs amusement parks use to build large circular theaters where they show a movie from all angles to make it look like you're in the middle of the action, just on a smaller scale."

"I don't understand," said Raven.

"Well imagine this: You have a room in your house that you can go into and turn on a projection. Suddenly you are bathed in bright but non-threatening light. The projection starts and you are surrounded by a field of tall prairie grass. In the distance you see a stand of trees. The projection moves and you feel as if you are walking toward the trees. Then you are walking through the trees, the lighting shifted by computer to put shadows into the room. Sounds of bugs and birds mingle with the rustle of trees. A startled fox runs away, bounding through the field. Fans controlled by the same computer that handles the lighting blows a breeze and a little scent added in makes the fantasy complete."

"Oh my God," said Raven, her tone hushed.

"Sounds like you might like it," Cowboy said. "So, how much would you pay for a room like that?"

"Anything you asked," said Raven. "I mean, that would be like heaven. Do you know how long it's been since I've been able to stand in a meadow like that?"

"About four hundred years for you, I reckon. Longer for others. And that's just one of the movies. I've also got movies of noon-time walks through the streets of New York, London, and Paris available with more in progress," he said.

Cowboy pulled to the curb, parking a half block from Raven's building. The conversation paused while Raven led him to her apartment. Once inside she felt it was safe to talk again.

"Cowboy, you must be raking it in. How come I haven't heard of this before?"

"Well you haven't exactly been sending me change of address notifications," he said. "I got into town a couple of weeks ago to build a few rooms for some of the well-heeled vampires out here. I built a couple dozen in Austin, and the word started to spread. I've been traveling about the country, selling and building my rooms. The last few months I've been out east, the New York City area."

"So you didn't just come out see me?" Raven asked, pouting at Cowboy.

"No, sorry. I didn't know you were here. I happened to spot a flyer for the club stapled to a phone pole and saw your face staring out at me. Sure, you changed your hair color and style, but I can never forget that lower lip."

Raven gave him a playful slap on his shoulder. "Down boy, I don't know if I've forgiven you for the scare you gave me back at the club."

Raven watched as Cowboy smiled at her. She remembered what about him had first attracted her to him all those decades ago.

"So, New York City," Raven said.

"Yes," said Cowboy, "and before you have to ask, yes Demetri is still there. No, I didn't see him, but I hear things."

"What can you tell me?" asked Raven.

"For one, Demetri has grown in power. His plan of banding together seems to be working. He's built up a power base among most of the vampires there, but has fingers into the pies of some of the normals, both legal and not."

"So he has succeeded," Raven said.

Cowboy seemed to consider her statement. "Yes and no. No one can remember the last time a vampire hunter was seen in Manhattan. Or rather the last time a live one was seen. He's established a power base so what he wants done gets done."

"But?"

"But his base is *only* in the New York City area. He's got some links with other vampires in the surrounding states that he has helped set up similar organizations," said Cowboy.

"Sounds like he's set up organized crime for vampires," Raven said.

"It does seem that he's using the mafia as a model."

"But you and I both know he doesn't want to just be the next Marlon Brando," Raven said.

"No, his sights are higher."

"King of the world is just a bit higher, that's for sure. After bringing all the vampires under his control, Demetri will next use us to bring the normals under his rule as well."

Cowboy was shaking his head while staring at the ground. "It's amazing the ambition you can put into play when you're immortal."

Raven got up and walked around the room, thinking about how much progress Demetri had made since she had left. "Is that what you came to tell me?"

"Not exactly," said Cowboy.

"What else is there?" asked Raven.

"Remember my construction business?" Cowboy asked. "Well it's amazing what people will talk about around the 'help.' A few months ago I overheard a conversation that you might be interested in."

"Spit it out, Cowboy. What did you hear?"

"Demetri is looking for you. Not just keeping an eye out. He is actively looking for you. He has sent agents out and they are looking for you all over the country. He wants you brought to him."

CHAPTER TWO

Jim was thinking he might just get to liking this Goth thing as he watched the redhead's boobs bounce and jiggle. She was definitely made for this dance. A few more minutes of this and he might forget what he'd come here for.

A man had to have his priorities straight.

Before he could decide that someone else should hunt down the scum of the earth, a large, hairy behemoth jumped up beside the redhead, snaking an arm around her to pull her close so they could slide up and down against each other. The redhead looked at Jim like she was laughing at him for his stupidity. The ugly behemoth's glare shouted louder than words, "My woman, back off."

Having been chosen for this assignment not for his strength or intelligence, but rather because of his all-American, innocent-hick good-looks, Jim gave them his best shucks-y'all-I-was-just-being-friendly, lopsided grin. They disappeared into the swirling, jumping crowd. Jim sighed. Looked like he'd be working tonight after all.

He scanned the crowd again, searching for vampire tells. He'd picked up what he'd thought was a couple of tells from the band earlier, but he'd been unable to get any closer to check them out for certain. He'd have to wait until they took a break. Maybe he could buy them a drink or something. He had to get up close to them, get them talking to him one-on-one, face-to-face, before he could be certain.

Jim suspected the tells were coming from the drummer. She seemed intense on her drums, almost in a primitive oneness with the rhythm. He hoped not, she was the type he could really go-for. Especially if that primitive oneness with rhythm spilled over into other parts of her life.

Sighing, Jim bounced around the room, searching for that indefinable something that indicated he should take a closer look. The band announced their break before he could sniff out anything else.

And to think Vic had assured him they'd find a vampire here at the club. Vic seemed to think the place, and by extension all Goths, were a hot-bed breeding-ground for vampires. To Jim, they just seemed like you're average club crowd.

The band didn't come out to get any drinks, so Jim figured he'd have to get backstage to check if the drummer was a vampire. Or get her phone number. Whichever seemed most appropriate.

The bouncer was also your basic club bouncer. Much larger than Jim, but not one wit more intelligent.

"C'mon man. I just gotta talk to them." Jim gave

the big guy a wide-eyed hick-in-the-headlights look. "I just wanna tell them that this has been the greatest night of my life. Everything's changed. It's something deep. My soul is changed."

"Forget it, kid," the bouncer said, pushing Jim back away from the door.

Just them a door down the hallway opened, and the band emerged, ready to start the next set. Jim shoved the bouncer and tried to squeeze past him. The singer looked back at him, but she didn't seem nearly as friendly as the drummer. Maybe she could get him past the bouncer.

"I have to see you." Jim tried to look unthreatening, and not to choke on the arm the bouncer pushed into his throat. "I want to talk to you—" He couldn't get out the rest, the arm on his throat effectively stopped all sound.

"Buy a ticket like everyone else, kid."

In seconds, Jim found himself in the dark staring at the wrong side of the stage door, and rubbing his throat.

Well, that hadn't gone nearly as well as he'd hoped. Maybe he wasn't cut out for this vampire hunter thing. His best lines, best faces, and best efforts had gotten him nowhere.

Just like going clubbing without hunting for vampires.

Figuring he owed Vic and the others another try, Jim returned to the dance floor. He'd circulate one last time, and if nothing came up he'd head out. The others would just have to accept his word that there weren't any vampires here.

Or they'd lose him, and get someone else to check the place and confirm that this wasn't a vampire hangout.

Nearing a shadowy spot where one of the lights had burned out, Jim felt the hairs on the back of his neck stand up. He passed by a slim girl swaying in the darkest part of the shadow. She didn't look old enough to be out this late. She wore a black leather jacket over a T-shirt. The color wasn't unusual, but the jacket was. The dance floor in the club had to be hotter than a kitchen.

He eased his way in a wide elliptical orbit that would allow him to look her over from all sides without being observed. She kept the jacket on, kept dancing, but she wasn't sweating. Pale, pale skin, accented by deep eyes, and the dark clothes were all he could make out at the farthest point away from her. The eyes though, they burned like stars, brighter than her skin. As he drew closer he checked her hands. Long painted nails topped fingers that were much too slender, and he could see no sign of veins on the backs of her hands. He'd need to be closer to check if he could see a pulse on her neck.

Circling in, he smiled tentatively at her. She watched him. Most girls would look away, either as a go-away signal, or only momentarily to check if he was really interested. She acted like she knew his every move. She had to be older than she looked.

"Uh, hi," he mumbled as he got close enough to talk. He smiled, aw-gee-shucks-ma'am. He looked away shyly. "I'm new here."

"That's obvious," she said, barely glancing at him.

"I'm Jim." He look up as far as her neck, as if too shy to look her in the eyes. No pulse that he could see. "You're... you're beautiful," he blurted and looked quickly at his feet before glancing up at her. That almost always hooked them.

And she did rise to the bait, she actually smiled at him. "That's one I haven't heard in a while."

"I probably shouldn't have said that," he drawled, daring to look into her eyes, golly-gee-shucks.

"You should always say what you think. When you think it." She nodded at him in time with the beat. "Especially if you're attracted to someone."

"Really?" Jim dropped his act and his dance, staring at her in open-mouthed wonder.

"Of course."

"Are you attracted to me?"

"No."

Of course not. Jim sighed, and started dancing again. Now he really did feel like the goof he was acting. Oh well, it didn't matter. He was here on a mission. And she looked like she fit the profile.

"Would you like to dance?" Jim didn't need to act like he couldn't dance as he bounced around. He really couldn't keep a beat, so that took no acting skill whatsoever. However, she didn't need to know that.

"We already are."

"Oh." He bopped around. All he needed to do now was to get her somehow attached to him, so that she'd follow him out.

"I'm, Jim." He extended his hand as if to shake hers.

"You said that already."

She didn't give him her hand, so he couldn't tell if it was cold or warm. Darn. He shrugged, and tried to look hang-dog. "What's your name?"

"Lucrecia"

"Cool name."

She sighed.

"I really like this band."

"Yes, they're good." She looked piercingly at him. "Do you know anything about them?"

"I almost met them a little bit ago, backstage." Well sort of. "But they had to get on for their last set."

"Really?" She seemed to alternate her attention between the band and Jim as they danced. Jim kept his eyes on her. Yup, she was definitely a vampire. Vic had been right. Now if only . . .

"What do you know about the lead singer?" she asked.

"Raven?" he asked, remembering the name from the billboard outside and searching his mind for a plausible lie. "She's okay. Great singer. I know more about the drummer, Tina, though. We used to live in the same neighborhood."

"Could you get both of us backstage?" The woman smiled at him, showing only the barest hint of tooth.

He stared at her mouth, as if infatuated with her every move. He could just make out the outline of a fang at the curve of her stretched lips. "Sure. Let me go talk with the bouncer."

This was too easy. She'd attached herself to him, rather than making him do the work. He recognized the pull of attraction as her working her vamp wiles on him, but he was prepared. He didn't know, or care,

what her interest was in the singer. He just had to alert
the troops to be in position for the ambush. The band
ended their set to the applause and screams of the
crowd. The noise would help his ruse.

Jim pulled his cell phone out as he approached the
bouncer. "Just gotta make a call, man."

The bouncer rolled his eyes.

Keeping his back to the vampire Goth, and looking
straight at the bouncer, Jim sent the message on his
cell. He smiled, just a normal smile, no gee-shucks.
"Thanks, man. I owe you one."

Heading back to Lucrecia, Jim smiled and waved
to her, feeling victorious. This was actually going to
work.

"So is it arranged?" she asked.

"Oh sure," he waved his hand. Glancing up at the
stage, he saw the band dismantling the drum set.
"They just gotta their gear packed. We're supposed to
meet them out back."

The way the building was built and huddled up
next to others on the block "out back" could only be
reached through a circuitous route, and was nowhere
near the stage entrance the band would be using.

"We've got a few minutes. How about I buy you a
drink?" Jim motioned over to the bar.

"No thanks." Lucrecia started heading toward the
front door. "Let's be early."

Sighing, Jim slouched after her. What was it with
women? He showered and shaved. He wasn't ugly,
didn't dress like a dork, had a job, tried to be polite,
and actually spent time trying to figure out and
provide whatever it was that women wanted. Yet,

most of them wouldn't give him the time of day.

Apparently not even vampire women.

Outside, the only light came from the garish neon sign above the club, and a few other storefronts. The streetlights at either corner had been shot out at sometime in the recent past. A few tiny diamonds of glass lay around the street corners. The neighborhood wasn't bad, it was just old and neglected.

Lucrecia waited impatiently for him in the shadow cast by the corner of one of the club's display front windows. The area had been a thriving shopping district back in the early twentieth century. Now the converted stores held restaurants, doctors and insurance offices, and a shaky art school.

Pointing down the street, Jim said, "We have to go down a bit to get to the alley."

He offered her his arm, but she ignored him. He walked slowly, it would take the other vampire hunters a few minutes to arrive. This was supposed to be an ambush. Jim certainly didn't want to find himself alone, in a proverbial dark alley, with a vampire. Or worse, with one that was beginning to suspect him.

The alley was in fact, nothing more than a pass through between two buildings. The footing was treacherous due to the cracked and buckled cement that was supposed to pass for a sidewalk, and trash had piled up, crackling and crunching underfoot. The worst stuff squelched and slid and stunk.

"Sorry," Jim said, turning back to watch Lucrecia picking her way through a particularly nasty patch. He couldn't see what they were stepping on in the near blackness between the buildings, but she seemed to know where to set her foot simply by concentrating. "It's kinda messy here. We could go the longer way if you'd prefer."

"Whatever you can handle, I can handle," she assured him.

She'd reached him, but he didn't move while he thought. Taking the long way would buy time for the others to get into position. Jim mentally kicked himself for not thinking of that earlier. He didn't want her to think he was afraid, but he was supposed to be leading them.

"Well?" she asked.

"I'm thinking."

Her teeth gleamed in the darkness as she laughed.

"It's just that there's something particularly smelly up ahead," he added lamely. Sometimes it felt like he really didn't have to act to be a goof.

Her hand reached out to grasp his arm and her slender form brushed against his as she leaned past him to sniff the air. While not exactly his type, Jim still liked the feel of her body against his. Another part of his mind reminded him of his duty, and the fact that her hand and her body were cold. Cold.

"Smells like four-day-old fast food burgers and fries," she said.

"What, no soda?" He wondered whether to put his arms around her, or squeeze back against the brick wall behind him. After all, the bricks would probably be warmer than her.

Lucrecia laughed again. "No soda." Her intense eyes looked up at him, and she moved to press herself up against him completely. "What, aren't you going to try your luck?"

"Uh." It would be in keeping with his idiot yokel act, but Jim had no interest in becoming vampire food. He tentatively started to put his arms around her.

She pushed past him, continuing down the alley. "Come on. I say we forge ahead. You'll just have to pinch your nose shut."

Jim sighed. He'd lost again, somehow.

The buildings were on what was often described as thin lots. The building was longer than it was wide so as to fit more stores onto one street. However, it only took them a few more moments to emerge into the alley proper.

By the way she kept looking around, it was clear she'd expected the alley to parallel the street. Not end up here.

The alley paralleled the street only a short way back toward the club, but ended abruptly in a ninety-degree turn. Beyond that it split in two heading apparently away from the club.

"Which way?" she asked impatiently.

Here actually, but he couldn't tell her that. The rest of the party hadn't arrived. "Just a moment," he said, thinking of a way to stall. "I gotta get this stuff off my shoes."

Making a great show of scraping his shoe this way and that across the rough bricks, Jim tried to make enough noise to cover for any footsteps that might be approaching them. He kicked and slashed his foot back and forth, up and down, pausing occasionally to catch his balance.

He turned to find Lucrecia watching him

incredulously. He nodded as he noticed a head peer out from behind a dumpster at the fork in the alley. "Okeydokey. Shall we?" He motioned for her to follow him.

"We take the left fork," he said conversationally, hoping she didn't notice the rustling down the right side. "And it'll curve back in just a bit. Not far now." She couldn't know this was a blatant lie, but he knew the attack would come just as the buildings narrowed onto the alley.

Jim's nerves were stretched to the breaking point when Vic, Lewis, Woo, Ken, and Matt jumped out in front of them. A quick glance behind them showed Ekson, Stevo, Truck, Pete, and Mike. Matt held what looked like a gun pointed at Lucrecia, who'd dropped into a fighting stance. The gun appeared to be shaking as Matt tried to hold it with one hand while his other hand fiddled with a dial on the side of the handle. No matter what he did it seemed to have no effect. Jim wondered if maybe Vic should've used it.

Lucrecia charged the five men blocking their path. Matt quickly backed out of the way, keeping his weapon pointed at Lucrecia. Woo and Lewis met her charge. Woo ducked under her first kick, but Lewis was unable to dodge her right fist and ended up slumped against the bricks. Her second kick caught Woo on the chin, knocking him back into Vic. Vic stood Woo up beside him to face Lucrecia.

Stopping for a moment, Lucrecia stood straight and wiggled one finger in her ear, as if she'd gotten water in it. "A sound gun? What's that supposed to do?"

"This isn't working," Matt said. He turned the gun to

better examine it, and a swath of brick dust exploded from a newly formed slash on the bricks of the building beside him. "Sorry."

Jim and Lucrecia were left coughing brick dust.

Suddenly Lucrecia jerked and collapsed onto the pavement. Mike grinned, and held up his taser. "Electricity still works."

"Jim you stay here with her, and we'll get the van," Vic said as he started away down the alley.

"Wait!" Jim ran after them. "What if she wakes up?"

Mike handed him the taser.

Jim waited in the darkness, torn between worry that he was alone, and a deeper worry that he wasn't.

He didn't have long to wait before he heard voices coming from the wrong direction. He drew back deeper into the shadows.

Four Goths were taking the same route he and Lucrecia had. The busty redhead and the hairy behemoth were too wrapped up in each other to notice Lucrecia lying in the shadow by the building, but their companions—a couple with enough chains hanging on their pants to almost cover the black—did notice.

The girl in the chain pants knelt down beside Lucrecia, feeling for a pulse at her neck. "I think she's dead."

"She doesn't look hurt," her boyfriend said. "There's no blood."

"Maybe she had a heart attack?" the busty redhead said.

"She's too young," the crouching girl said.

"Call the police," he hairy behemoth said.

The young man with the chains pulled out his cell phone, pressed a few buttons, and held it to his ear. "Uhm. We found this woman. We think she may be dead. She has no pulse."

Before Chain Goth could give any specifics, Jim backed farther into the darkness, heading the way the others had gone to get the van. He met them coming back, and explained what had happened.

"Get in the van," Vic said. "We'll take care of it."

"But they might recognize me. They were at the club," Jim said as he got in.

"So don't get out of the van."

It seemed to Jim that Vic never worried.

The van drove quickly through the alley to where the four Goths still waited by the unconscious body of the vampire Lucrecia.

Vic jumped out of the van before it had completely stopped. "All right, everyone get back." He walked briskly toward the Goths, pausing only to look back at the others getting out of the van. "You two," he pointed to Truck and Stevo, "get statements, and make it fast, we've got to get her to the M.E. as quickly as possible."

From his hiding spot, almost in the exact center of the van, it was hard for Jim to see exactly what was going on, or to hear either. Vic disappeared from view as he knelt down by the unconscious vampire.

Truck, who made the hairy behemoth look tiny, helped Stevo herd the Goths away, back far away. The Goths appeared to be complaining, and Jim could hear Stevo shout, "We *are* the police. Plainclothes." He said something more, but Jim couldn't make out what it was. They stood with the four, blocking the Goths from seeing what was going on with the unconscious vampire.

Vic, Pete, Ekson, and Ken picked up the body. It seemed strange to Jim that it would take all four of them to pick up so slight a girl, but then Jim remembered they had to be pretending to carry her on a stretcher. When they reached the van, Jim helped them get her settled into the seat prepared for her and strapped down firmly.

"Mike, get over here." Vic took the taser from Jim and handed it back to Mike as Mike crawled into the van. "Sit beside her, if she so much as stirs, shoot her."

Then Vic headed for the driver's seat, shouting, "Come on."

"What about our statements?" the Goth girl with all the chains on her pants yelled.

"We'll get them later," Truck yelled back.

"You're not cops," the girl shouted. "Who are you?"

Vic already had the van started, and drove off without answering her. The four Goths started to run after the van, but couldn't keep up. In the distance they heard sirens getting closer.

Laughing, Vic said, "Well, if they did call the cops, they're going to be in trouble now. Cops hate responding to prank calls."

"What if the cops believe them?" Jim asked.

Vic snorted. "The cops aren't going to believe a bunch of stupid Goths. Trust me."

"What if they tell the cops about us?" Jim asked.

"Nobody is going to believe them." Vic swung the

van onto the freeway, driving like a maniac. "You worry too much."

Mike nudged Jim to keep him quiet.

"This new machine had better work," Woo said from the back of the van, where he was rubbing his head.

"Not like the sound gun," Truck said.

"No, no." Matt put the sound gun carefully back in its case. "Sound doesn't seem to affect them, but the new machine doesn't use sound. I'm sure you'll be pleased with my demonstration. Now that we have an appropriate test subject."

There was something peculiar about the way Matt smiled, as he caressed the case in his lap. His eyes were a little too crazy for Jim's taste.

"You'll be really impressed with what my machine can do."

CHAPTER THREE

Demetri stood before the large bay window of his penthouse apartment, staring down at night enshrouded Manhattan Island. The lights of the city twinkled up at him. He loved this city. The hum of humanity that never stopped. The constant activity that acted as a pulse, the automotive and pedestrian traffic flowing through the arterial roads to sustain the life of the city. They were commerce. They were life. They were power.

He knew he was born for this age. He had lived for a thousand years to get here, but it was as if he had always been waiting for the world to catch up. Even a hundred years ago the technology didn't exist that now allowed him to maintain an ever-widening empire. Centuries of skulking in shadows, hiding from even those of his own kind that he had not brought into the dark, planning.

But Demetri had planned well. He had learned to work within the laws and rules of the normals. At first he had been forced to hire them, pay them their script of paper with portraits of dead men to get what he needed. It galled him. More than once he discovered deceit and theft from those hired to protect him from such activity. The confrontation with the thieves always provided him an opportunity to feed, but it also faltered his plans.

It was when he had grown tired of the petty deceits of the normals that Demetri started on his current method of moving his plan forward. Instead of hiring normals, Demetri sought out those he could use and transformed them to the higher plane. Once they were vampires Demetri was able to command their loyalty without question. Once on his side of the sun line they were as eager as he to work for his final goal, when vampires would openly rule the "normals."

There was still a ways to go, but when he looked down on the city he imaged a time when it would openly be his.

"Sir."

Demetri turned to his assistant. "What is it, Marc?"

"They're all here, in the conference room."

"About time," said Demetri as he checked the time on his watch.

There were two problems that Demetri had to accept with grace when dealing with vampires. It seemed that no matter what kind of human they were before they were changed, once they were vampires each became an individualist. Even though Demetri had convinced them that his long term goals were the only way to go, it seemed they had to assert their individuality in minor ways. One was their disregard for being on time for meetings.

Demetri stepped into the conference room and was reminded of the other. Clothing. While he preferred the look and cut of a dark Italian suit, those in his inner circle varied in styles from Goth casual, to all leather, all the way to the formal evening wear Hollywood had inflicted on the world as expected vampire attire.

Looking around the table at the nine members of his inner circle, Demetri knew at least that they were loyal. He had worked with polished yes-men before with poor results. With this group he had assembled the cornerstone to build his empire.

"Thank you for all coming," Demetri said as he took his seat at the head of the table. "It shouldn't be any surprise to any of you that we are close to being able to consolidate our control over our population on this continent."

There were nods around the table. It was something they discussed often enough.

"Stephen, what's the latest on hunters?" Demetri asked.

Two seats down the table on his left Stephen cleared his throat before beginning. "We've been able to identify seventeen hunter gangs operating in the US and Canada. We think there may be four more in Mexico, but we haven't been able to confirm them yet. We're ready to take out the known gangs at any time."

Demetri shook his head. "No. Remember what I said."

"You said to make them ineffectual," said Stephen. "By sending in a dozen of our people we should be able clear out a nest pretty fast."

"And then what happens?" Demetri asked.

"Sir?"

"Exactly. You don't know what happens next," Demetri said. "If we take out the entire hunter gang, another one will rise in its place once the feeding of our people gets under their skin. The loners out there can't help but leave clues as to their existence."

Demetri paused and looked around the table. "But what if we identify the leaders of these groups and take only them out?"

"They'd come after us even harder," Stephen said.

"They would if they thought we had done it," Demetri said. "But if they die in accidents, and not all the leaders of each group all at once. Traffic accidents, home invasions gone bad, or perhaps a cross bow bolt from one of their own weapons while out on a hunt?"

When no one provided an answer, Demetri continued. "If their best leaders are killed, the people that move up in the organizations will be less skilled. The human hunters think we are cowards and hide from them just because we can't go out in the light of day. We will use that to our advantage. We can track them, learn who they are, and if any of their members get too good, we remove them with the precision of a skilled surgeon."

Now the heads were nodding again, a little more vigorously. They were also smiling. There was nothing so empowering as striking back at an enemy who is oblivious that the attack has occurred.

"Stephen, I want you to identify the leader of the five most active hunter gangs and devise an accident that is unique to each of them," Demetri said.

"Yes, sir," Stephen said while scribbling down notes on the pad of paper in front of him.

"Now, what is going on in Dallas and Chicago? Jenny?"

A woman in a short-skirted, blue business suit and spiky blonde hair sitting half way down the right side of the table spoke. "Dallas is going forward as planned and on schedule. Our teams weren't able to discover any sort of organized vampire groups in the area."

"Excellent," said Demetri.

Jenny continued. "During the search they did identify a vampire that most of the other vampires seemed to defer to. Following your guidelines they spoke with her about setting up an organization with our financial and other support."

"What was her response?" asked a vampire slouching across from Jenny.

Demetri looked down the table at the vampire who spoke, Adam. He was dressed in jeans and an AC/DC T-shirt. He was young, both as a human and as a vampire. He had been converted only a few years ago. He had a tendency to be petulant and a bore. If it wasn't for his knowledge of computers and the networks that connect them, Demetri would never have brought him over, let alone make him part of his inner circle. Adam knew that knowledge was power, and thought he had a lot based on his knowledge. Demetri let him maintain that world view. But Demetri knew that true power came from how knowledge was harnessed and used. The fact that Adam worked for Demetri was proof of that.

"She goes by the name Cassandra Night, and she was

interested," said Jenny, looking at Demetri. "She liked the idea of support and protection in dealing with the hunters. Most of our people have been living on the fringes down there."

"Good," said Demetri. "We should be able to build a bond of trust from the beginning with her. Those that have had to live with a lower quality of life tend to appreciate it more when things get better."

Demetri made eye contact with the vampire next to Jenny. His name was Richard and he appeared to be a human male in his mid-fifties. He had salt and pepper hair and looked to be about forty pounds over weight. Demetri knew the weight was the result of extra padding in his suit.

Years before when Demetri had discovered this fact, Richard had explained to him that the padding served two purposes. The first was street scum liked to pick on victims they thought were easy targets. Richard always loved the fear that shown in their eyes when the fat old man turned out to be twice as strong as them and not satisfied with just letting them get away. He always fed so that he made eye contact. Richard liked to watch hope drain from their eyes, then fear leave, and finally their life. The second purpose was that it provided some extra protection if a hunter caught up with him.

"Richard, how are our brothers and sisters in Chicago?"

"There's not much of a change I'm afraid," Richard said. "The three groups of vampires are still stalling. There have been no steps to merge their organizations."

"You gave each group my ultimatum? Told them how they had to fit in now to be a part of the larger plan?"

"Yes," said Richard.

"So, what did they say? I can't believe that all three groups that have been fighting among themselves for fifty years as well as fighting the hunters can't see the power behind a single local organization backed by an international conglomerate."

Richard shook his head. "I agree. The problem seems to be that each group thinks it should be the dominant one and control the other two."

"I see," said Demetri. He leaned back in his chair, rocking slowly, his index fingers tapping together in front of his face. He had to take action at this point. But he needed it to be such that destroying one group would bring the other two into line.

"Richard, what is the name of the vampire in charge of the second strongest group in Chicago?"

"Nero Walsh."

Demetri looked down the table to the vampire sitting at the foot of the table. "Gunther, I want you to go to Chicago and work with Nero Walsh to take out the more powerful organization. You know the routine. Booby trap hideouts, work with hunters, even get the normals' government involved. Like we did down in DC."

"Why not use the more powerful group to wipe out the other two?" asked Adam.

Demetri sighed. He was getting tired of having to explain himself. "Because if the stronger group is left in power, how long do you think it would be until they decide they want to take us over? By helping Nero destroy his long time enemy we earn his loyalty. Plus, he knows that he is put in charge at our pleasure, and that if he gets out of line we won't have any qualms about doing the same to him."

"And the third group?" Adam asked.

"They'll see what happened to the others. Shortly after the Nero's group has taken out the other, they will be issued an invitation to join Nero and his group. No request to discuss merging or sharing power. They will join or be without the benefit of our protection, shall we say."

Demetri looked around the table, gauging their reaction to what had to be done. "Are there any more reports in our expansion areas? No one? Good. Next month we'll begin with the major cities on the west coast."

Some of the vampires began to rise from their seats. Demetri waved them back down.

"We're not done yet," he said. "I want to go over the reports from our operatives searching for Khalida Raven."

Everyone settled back into their seats.

Demetri looked around the table, making eye contact with each individual. "We've had operatives working in every city we've brought under our control, and dozens more in other cities we are planning to pursue. Are you telling me that we have nothing?"

The silence extended until the woman next to him spoke. "No one has seen her, Demetri. We've worked with the others in every city we can. We've had drawings made of her in varying hairstyles.

Nothing."

"Then we must try other options," Demetri said.

"It's not exactly like we can hire a private detective to search for her like a human missing person," said Adam.

Demetri cocked his head to the side, extending Adam's comment to the next level of a plan. "Don't we have some former members of police departments and other law enforcement organizations?" he asked.

"Yes," said Richard.

"Then lets put them to work on this. Remember my direction in setting this group up. Never rely on a normal when we can use our own kind."

Richard cleared his throat. "We have, and they've tried. The problem is that their experience is based upon when they were, uh, normal. The norms have extensive databases with electronic tendrils that crisscross the globe to identify and track their people. But these are best served for finding people who aren't hiding. The people living ordinary lives are easily identified, cross referenced, and we can find out where they ate breakfast last Tuesday, what they had, how they paid the check, and what kind of tipper they are. But these software behemoths have trouble tracking normals that don't want to be found and go underground."

"And a vampire with centuries of experience moving through society undetected is going to be even harder," said Adam. "Even the internet sites that allow every Bubba in Buttscratch, Arkansas to find out hidden secrets about their new neighbors need a starting point. Trust me, I've entered Khalida's name in each of them."

Demetri tapped his fingers rhythmically on the table. His mind was racing, trying to find a course of action. He had to have her with him and no cost was too great. Agitated he stood and began pacing.

"Correct me if I'm wrong, Demetri, but hasn't Khalida been gone a long time? We really don't need her to move forward and take control," said Adam.

Demetri stopped and turned his body so he was facing Adam directly. He was pleased to see the others pull back.

"Young Adam, I am going to make a prediction about you. More specifically about how you will die," Demetri said.

"Uh, sure," said Adam.

"I predict that you are going to die by being struck by lightning."

The puzzled look that crossed Adam's face was gratifying. He needed an inner circle that felt close to him, but Demetri needed to be feared. He needed for them to always remember that it was he who was destined to rule. Each of them could be replaced, but if he were to be killed they would cease to be an organization and return to loners skulking in the shadows.

"I say this, Adam, because you are a lightning rod," said Demetri, his voice low and his tone very even. "You say things without thinking them through to see the impact your words will have on those around you. You take on the trappings and attitude of a street punk. But think about what happens to those street punks."

Demetri leaned forward on the table and looked into Adam's eyes. "They die young."

Standing again, Demetri continued to speak. He directed his words to Adam as the others tried to blend into the background, but he wanted the others to hear them.

"Power is partially about perception. I know who I am and what I am destined for. But there are many out there who do not. Our organization is in the process of educating those of our kind. Some catch my vision and join our legions." Demetri began to pace again, taking slow measured steps around the table.

"Others do not get a clear vision. They fight us. They hide and kick at the tendrils of sunlight until it consumes them and they are no longer a problem."

"I understand," said Adam.

Demetri stopped Adam with a raised index finger.

"Tell me Adam, who is Khalida Raven?"

"She's your first. I mean she's the one you converted first," said Adam.

"No, that is incorrect," said Demetri. "The thing to remember about the mantra of your human childhood of 'knowledge is power,' is that first you must have knowledge. You have demonstrated why you didn't have the power to not ask your earlier question. Had you the knowledge that Khalida is not my first but rather my oldest living convert you might have seen the greater significance of my need for her.

"How would it look if she were to side against me with a rival? What would the perception be to others? What would they think is the reality?" Demetri said, raising his voice to a shout as he spoke.

"I think I understand," said Adam, his voice quieter, without the bluster he had shown earlier.

"Good," said Demetri as he sat back in his seat. "It has occurred to me that we may not have been utilizing all of our options in our search for Khalida."

"What other options do we have?" asked Richard.

"It's possible that she hasn't taken up residence in a city. Perhaps she is hiding out in smaller towns."

Richard pursed his lips, an expression that Demetri had come to understand that Richard was in deep analysis of the statement.

"I don't know how we can find her if that is true," said Richard. "Even with a thousand operatives it would take us years to work across the country. And that assumes she doesn't move around."

"No, Richard, you are looking at the problem the wrong way. Rather than sending agents to comb the backwoods, let's use young Adam's specialty," Demetri said as he nodded toward Adam.

"What do you need me to do?" asked Adam.

"We may not be able to find a vampire who wants to stay hidden, but all vampires feed. We need to find evidence of her feedings. Sure, we'll get a lot of others, but it might give us some hot spots to sent agents into."

Demetri waited with the others while Adam looked off into the distance.

"Yes," said Adam, speaking while still staring at the wall over their heads. "I can set up a search bot to access online news venues for unexplained deaths and disappearances. Even the smallest Podunk paper has a web site these days. We can sift through the hits and look for trends or obvious vampire activity."

"Excellent," said Demetri. "But let's not back off on our efforts currently underway. Let us adjourn now. The sun will be up soon."

Demetri was pleased. Not only had a new direction been implemented that might soon bring his Khalida back to him, but he got the opportunity to slap down that impertinent pup. He was glad that he had been able to chastise Adam while finding a way at the same meeting to bring his talent to the forefront and make him feel useful. The touch of a ruler—make them fear, then a gentle touch. The gentle touch they remembered on the surface of their skin. The fear they remembered in their blood.

CHAPTER FOUR

The mansion had once belonged to someone rich. That had been a long time before Vic got a hold of it. Now it was just an over-large, tumbledown house in desperate need of new plumbing, new heat, new roof, new wiring, new carpet, patching on the plaster, a good coat of paint, and someone to do something about the weeds in the yard. Probably, Jim thought, it'd just be best to tear the monstrosity down and start fresh.

Vic didn't care about all that. He only cared about vampire hunting. The rest of the gang hung around with him for their own various reasons. Truck was just looking for violence that wouldn't get him in too much trouble. Truck wasn't alone there, most of the rest also liked the violent aspect of the hunt, and the fact that there wouldn't be much trouble. Vampires didn't go complaining to the police, and their bodies were easily turned to ash. But there were other reasons along with the violence.

They all liked being part of the crowd and having

a roof over their heads. They liked feeling important, feeling like they were doing something to make the world a little better for everyone. They were heroes, even if no one knew it.

Then, of course, they each had some kind of run in with a vampire in the past.

Every time they killed a vampire Jim wondered if he finally avenged his sister. If he'd finally managed to kill the monster that had made her over in its own image. But he didn't know. He would never know. Before her death he never managed to find out which vampire had done it. So now, as far as Jim was concerned, they all had to die.

To allow even one of the bastards to live after they'd trapped it seemed wrong, but Vic had promised Matt they'd capture one alive to use as a test subject for his new machine. So the vampire Lucrecia, now awake, remained unkilled, trapped in a cage of iron, silver, and steel bars in the center of the largest room on the top floor of the old mansion.

Jim consoled himself with the thought that she'd be dead soon. Very soon.

His greatest fear, all of the vampire hunters' greatest fear, was that some day he'd be bitten. That he'd one day become the enemy. Their exposure to the vampires made it a very real, occasionally realized, fear.

That fear also contributed to the cohesiveness of the gang. They'd all sworn that if one of their number was ever bitten, that member would be killed before anything else. Before anyone rested. Before anyone ate. Before revenge. Before the poor bastard could hurt anyone else.

Jim didn't know who Matt was doing this for, or what had caused him to seek out other vampire hunters, but there was something not-quite-right about the squirrelly little man.

Everyone could tell when Matt was thinking about killing vampires. His smile became strange and his eyes shone a tad too much. He was brilliant, possessing several degrees, obviously smarter than anyone else in the group. He constantly invented new ways of killing. Or maiming. Or incapacitating.

He unnerved all of them sometimes. Most of his inventions would work against normal people, but Matt insisted on destroying any that didn't work on vampires.

So as soon as they'd returned to the mansion, Matt had immediately begun dismantling the sound gun. Then he'd asked for help getting all the parts, notes, and books for his new machine up to the top floor in the room they'd chosen for the test. Jim wasn't sure exactly why, but somehow he'd been tapped to be Matt's assistant.

"Help me find the text for the laser sight," Matt said, as he piled another book onto Jim's already laden arms.

Jim looked around at the mess that was Matt's room. Everything had a label. Jim had almost expected to see a piece of paper taped to the bed that said "MATT MANN, BED," but instead the covers themselves were covered in writing, Matt's neat printed equations. Meaningless to Jim, but of obvious importance to Matt.

"Is that it?" Jim nodded to an overstuffed bookshelf.

On a green book the label "MATT MANN" almost obscured the title, which did include the words "Laser Sight."

"No," Matt said. "The one I'm looking for is my own work. It'll be in manuscript format."

That meant it would be among the various stacks of loose paper filling the room. Jim decided to just stand around looking stupid. And bored. There wasn't much to look at on the walls, The posters were all pictures of some type of invention, some covered in Matt's neat writing. Apparently Matt's interests ran to machines and mathematical equations, not big-breasted women in skimpy clothes.

Matt found what he was looking for halfway down one of the stacks on the seat of his desk chair. He loaded that onto the pile in Jim's arms. "Take that up, then come back and we can start shifting the rest of the computer parts up."

Times like this made Jim wonder if maybe he ought not to just conclude that probably his sister's murderer was dead. Maybe he should go back to his life. Find some pretty girl and, well not settle down, but have a little fun sometimes. Killing vampires got grim after a while.

The first time he'd staked one it'd been a thrill, the heat of the chase, the excitement of doing good, the thrill of revenge. Watching someone die for what had been done to his sister had been almost as good as sex. An orgasm of blood spurting around the stake, from the severed head, coupled with the relief of still being alive, of managing to take down something more powerful.

The second had been as good. And the third, and the fourth, and the fifth, and.... Then he'd discovered Vic and the other vampire hunters. Joined forces with them. The sheer slaughter after a while no longer thrilled him. Jim spent too much time thinking of his sister Tracey. Sometimes now when he staked a girl vampire he wondered if somewhere her family grieved for her. The thrill wasn't the same for him any more, but the knowledge that he'd finally put someone out of their misery, eased someone's grief kept him going.

Jim dropped his load onto the window seat. The vampire woman, Lucrecia, stood in the cage glaring at them. At least she'd stopped cursing. Most of the time she just stood there looking bored.

Everyone had expected she'd be scared when she woke up, but she hadn't been. She seemed to assume she'd escape somehow, and was obviously planning on taking as many of them with her as she could. Jim had no doubt he was on her list of those who would die, because every time he put in an appearance, she glared and growled particularly.

Not that Jim was all that worried. She was completely contained, and no one in this mansion would fall under her spell. He just itched to kill her. Slam a wooden stake in her heart, cut off her head, and leave her in the backyard for the sun to turn to ashes.

That was how things should be done. Jim didn't have much faith in Matt's machine. More than half of them didn't work. Vic believed in Matt, believed that someday Matt would come up with a weapon they could use to kill all vampires without worrying about hurting normal people.

In Vic's vision, someday they'd all have some kind of hand-held weapon, which would kill vampires but not bother anyone else, and not be noticed.

In Jim's mind, this translated into somehow blessing an entire weather system, and turning all the rain into holy water. Just not possible.

Still even Matt's misses were usually entertaining.

Back in Matt's room, Jim found several pieces of electronic equipment waiting for him. He'd have to make a third trip to bring the computer up. Jim sighed to himself as he performed his role as pack-mule. Why couldn't Matt have got himself a laptop rather than a desktop?

Maybe Matt was afraid he couldn't even lift a laptop.

Up in the upper room, Matt directed Jim in where to set the equipment. Matt connected it himself, though. They all remembered the time he'd expected Jim to help connect things. No one used that room anymore, the roof leaked too much.

Everything was carefully placed on a long table. One end of the table rested against a wall, the other end stopped just short of arm's reach from the vampire woman's cage. Jim didn't know what most of the equipment was, but Matt wanted it in a particular order on a particular side of the table. A surge-protector/extension cord ran down the middle of the table, supplying electricity to all the equipment.

In fact the whole middle of the table lengthwise was a no-mans-land of electrical cables. The room began to heat up and smell of ozone from the equipment.

The vampire woman continued to glare at everyone,

and growl whenever anyone got near, but didn't seem concerned in the least.

Jim guessed she had the same opinion of Matt's machine as he did.

Just before dawn, Matt said, "We'll need to black out all the windows in this room."

"How much longer is this going to take?" Vic asked.

"I need to retest every piece to make certain it wasn't broken on the trip up here, and then I need to double check that everything is connected properly in sequence." Matt patted the longest piece of his mysterious electrical equipment. "Then I need to do a smoke test, before we finally turn it on her."

"How long is all that going to take?" Jim asked, nearly shouting.

"I should have it all ready by noon."

Jim didn't realize he'd started toward Matt until Vic stepped in front of him blocking him. "Calm down." Vic turned to Matt. "We'll give you all the time you need. Just make sure this works." He started pushing Jim toward the door. "The rest of us will all get some sleep, and we'll plan on watching the test just after sundown tonight."

Truck and Stevo joined Vic, helping to push Jim out. Sputtering his protests, Jim had no choice but to exit the room. However once out he turned on Vic.

"What was that about? That vampire is still alive!" Jim shouted.

"Calm down." Vic's hands patted the air as if trying to calm Jim from a distance. "We *are* going to kill her."

"To live like that. Even a second." Jim shook with repressed anger. "It's wrong."

"I know. I know." Vic looked Jim in the eye. "I know. I understand. But this is bigger than anything else we've ever done. This might be it. Just this once. We've got her caged. It's not like she can hurt anyone."

Truck and Stevo said nothing, just stood behind Vic, waiting to see if Jim would need any extra restraint.

Seething with fury, Jim said, "You wouldn't coddle *me* like this if I wanted to keep a vampire alive."

"You can't do what he does." Vic shrugged. "I've never found anyone that can and will do what he does."

Swallowing his rage and frustration, Jim stalked off down the stairs toward his room.

"If it doesn't work, I promise I'll let you stake her," Vic shouted from the top of the stairs.

Jim growled quietly to himself. He'd just about had enough of this. The killings weren't the same. Living in this run-down, moldy hovel was only one step up from sleeping on the streets. And now this.

Vampires needed to be put out of their misery. Who would want to live like that? Undead, soulless, hungering for blood, living a life that only hurt themselves and others. No one would want that.

Leaving her alive, well undead, in the cage, wanting their blood, yearning unnaturally for it. That was wrong. Very, very wrong.

Well, this was it. Tonight. He'd had enough. If, probably when, Matt's machine didn't work, Jim decided he would leave, go home, go back to a normal life. Or at least as normal as he could manage at this point.

The chances that this machine would work at all were slim to none, and the chance that it might actually be the weapon of Vic's fevered imagination was nil.

If it was even close, Jim decided he'd stay. Not that it was very likely, but Jim wanted to be fair.

Packing his stuff up wouldn't take long. He had no dresser or closet. He'd just lived out of a laundry basket he'd acquired at some point. Packing was a matter of throwing the dirty clothes from his floor into the basket.

Jim threw himself onto the thin mattress resting on the floor, covered with a pile of blankets that served as his bed. He'd get some rest, then when Matt's latest machine didn't work, he'd stake the vampire they'd caught, and then he'd just go.

When they woke him for the test firing of the machine, it was already past sunset. Matt was still dithering over the machine when Jim walked into the room.

Vic looked him over. "You okay."

"Fine." Jim shrugged. "Just fine."

As expected, as soon as everyone was assembled Matt went into lecture mode.

"Vampires can be killed by one of several methods." Matt paced up and down the length of his table, unwilling to get near the caged vampire. "Staking them through the heart. Which," Matt conceded with a shrug, "also works on normal people." He ticked off a second finger. "Cutting off their heads. Again this works on ordinary people." He turned to head back, his hands whirling through the air to make his point. "So I wanted to find something that would kill only vampires, and leave regular people unharmed." He looked up at them as he turned back again. "That left sunlight, which burns them, and can eventually kill them by turning them to ashes." Turn. "And holy water, which also burns them." He was silent for a moment, eyes shining. Turn. "The light from an ordinary light bulb is not a problem for them. Our ordinary ultraviolet light bulbs might give them a headache, but nothing more." Turn. "And light and holy water have little effect on normal people."

"Sunburns and drowning come to mind," Mike said.

Vic glared at him, but Matt stopped his pacing and nodded. "True, true. Hopefully this test will help us to gain the next step in realizing the goal of the ultimate vampire fighting machine."

Resuming his pacing, Matt said, "What I have done with this machine is to combine a powerful laser that I have calibrated to alternate between the far ultraviolet and the infrared." He patted his computer. "I have a program set up here that I can tweak, or adjust, if one seems to work better than the other." Turn. "This computer will also record and calculate the results of the test." Turn. "The laser though," his hand skimmed the air above the longest piece of the arrayed electronics, "is the key as well as delivery system for my new machine, but I wanted to combine light with holy water, to obtain the best effects." He smiled and picked up a small goldfish-bowl sized glass container.

"This is what makes my machine special. Holy water." Matt carefully placed the water back into its spot in the configuration. "My machine uses laser light refracted through holy water to hopefully make the combination stronger than the parts."

"Holy laser light, Matt Mann!" Jim just couldn't resist.

Everyone turned to stare at him.

"Don't look at me," Jim said. "You were thinking it."

"Actually you're quite correct," Matt said into the accusatory silence. "Holy laser light."

Jim wondered if he didn't get the reference, or if he just didn't care.

Everyone turned their attention back to Matt.

"Everything is set up and properly tested and calibrated. The software is ready to go." Matt stationed himself beside his precious laser. "Vic if you would get the lights."

Jim glanced over at the vampire woman. She'd finally started to look worried, eyeing the set up on the table with doubt. Well, if she wasn't out of her misery soon from this infernal machine, Jim had sworn to make certain he put her out of her misery.

Vic turned the lights off. It took a moment for everyone's eyes to adjust to the light provided by the computer screen and the readouts on the rest of the equipment.

"Here we go." Matt started some program on his computer with a single click of his mouse, then began adjusting a few knobs on some of the other equipment.

At first there was nothing much to see. A bit of grating static-type noise filled the room as the laser powered up. Colors changed on a few dials and on the computer screen.

Jim expected to see a laser beam shoot from the laser to the woman, but nothing seemed to be happening.

"Look," Stevo said.

A small dot appeared on the woman, appearing to alternate between red and purple. She hadn't noticed it, and it seemed not to bother her at first.

As Matt muttered to himself his fingers flew over the keyboard, and he slung the mouse pointer across the screen. Jim didn't understand a word Matt was muttering.

Smoke began to coil up from spot of light on the vampire woman, and she jerked back to get away from it, looking frightened.

"Go Matt," Vic whispered.

Matt moved the laser a fraction, and the spot of light reappeared on the woman. She moved again. Matt moved the laser. She moved. Matt moved the laser.

Her clothes were riddled with tiny holes from the laser, and thin coils of smoke trailed from each little hole. She finally resorted to constant movement to avoid the laser.

With a strange smile on his face and eyes that shone far too much in the light of the computer display, Matt muttered something understandable. "Now the beauty part."

A single stamp by Matt's foot on a pedal on the floor

caused mirrors to open out from the bars of the cage. Matt now moved the laser to hit one of the mirrors.

Instead of bouncing the light back toward the laser, it bounced from one mirror to another, until the cage was encircled with a spiral of light. The thin trails of smoke were the only thing that revealed the light.

The woman had become frantic, trying desperately to deflect the mirrors and thus the light, but her efforts only succeeded in tightening the spiral.

Jim couldn't figure out how couldn't only manage to get the mirrors to go the wrong way, until he realized that the pedal at Matt's foot had some sort of adjustment on it. Matt was slowly, in time with her struggles, putting more pressure on the front of the pedal, as if driving a car.

Smoke and steam curled up from Lucrecia as the spiraling light enveloped her. She writhed and screamed in agony. Her hair lifted up and stood out from her head as if from some electrical field.

As Jim watched, fascinated, Matt made more adjustments on his computer and to several knobs. Jim expected the woman to burst into flames, as vampires would in the sun, and burn to ashes. Instead he was treated to a bizarre anatomy lesson.

Suddenly Jim saw her internal organs, then her skeleton, then her muscular system, then the whole woman. The smoke and steam obscured his vision somewhat, but she continued to jump back and forth through these odd appearances, all the while writhing and screaming.

The screaming had been a high pitched soprano, suddenly it dropped to a deep primal roar, reminding

Jim that there was no woman in that cage, only a monster. What he saw there looked like the statue of a woman made of congealed crimson blood, melting and dripping.

More adjustments by Matt, and not only did her appearance change as in an anatomy lesson, but her body seemed to bend and warp in ways impossible for human beings. Sometimes appearing to actually go out of the cage. Jim half expected to see blood dripping onto the floor.

"She can't escape this way, can she?" Vic asked Matt quickly.

"No, no." Matt didn't bother looking away from his work at the computer. "She isn't really bending that way, it's just the effects of the lights. Smoke and mirrors, you know."

From the extremely strange look on Matt's face, Jim wasn't sure if he should believe him.

Glancing from one of the electrical displays to the cage, Jim was able to see that Matt was controlling the way she looked. Now a curved wave, now a spiked wave, now static.

The cloying steam and smoke and heat made the room feel oppressive even to Jim. He worried that if this didn't kill her he might not have the energy to do the job himself.

The roar was slowly diminishing, along with the odd x-ray appearance, and weird shaping. The smoke and steam increased filling not only the cage but the rest of the room in a burst of heat. There was a final flickering as of a flame, then only the laser light standing out in the smoke and steam.

Vic turned the lights back on. Everyone stared in silence at the slowly clearing smoke.

There was nothing left in the cage. No ashes, no clothing. On the stone floor of the cage were a few congealing bits of melted metal, possibly from jewelry.

"Wicked," said Truck.

"Open a window," Vic ordered. Mike quickly flung the window open, letting the cool night air in to revive everyone.

"That was amazing," Stevo said. "I can't believe it. You did it Matt!"

Matt nodded, with a tight smile. "This time wasn't very efficient. I had to try out various combinations to discover what worked best. But next time, it'll be faster."

Vic grinned and slapped Matt's back. "That was awesome! You're definitely onto something with this."

"Oh, there's still problems," Matt said. "But I can see where I need to work now."

"Problems? What problems?" Vic crowed. "Render this thing down to something we can hold in our hands and I'd say it's open season on vampires."

"All right!" Mike shouted.

"That's the crux of the problem." Matt began powering down all his equipment, starting with the laser. "I can't go smaller. The laser loses power with diminishing size. I can go larger, but not smaller. The other problem is that any of us in there would have died also. Not like she did, but the laser would have burned us. If I held it on anyone long enough they'd catch fire." He looked critically at the holy water container. "Of course normal people wouldn't produce steam with the smoke, perhaps there is some way I could make some kind of feedback loop. No steam and the weapon shuts off." He trailed off in a thoughtful hum.

"But not smaller?" Vic asked.

"No. Sorry, not smaller." Matt pulled one of his manuscripts from the pile. "From previous testing I know that we can cause the equivalent of a sunburn on them with lesser lasers, but to get the a killing effect, we need a stronger laser. Those little laser pointers may frighten a vampire, but they just won't kill."

"So, what now?" Ken asked. "Do we have to drag all the vampires in L.A. up here?" He motioned around them.

"Oh no. No, no," Matt hurriedly said. "I think I can make it bigger, something we can put in a van, all we'd need to do would be put up a few carefully positioned mirrors. I could make them wireless controlled. And we could get a whole building full of vampires. An office, a club, a house. Something like that."

Jim thought about killing a whole houseful or clubful of vampires. Now that would be worth sticking around for.

CHAPTER FIVE

Raven woke and stretched, relishing in the movement and the feel of the soft cotton oversized nightshirt brushing against her skin. She was so glad the world had gone back to cottons. Just the thought of the years of polyester and other synthetics made her skin itch. Raven indulged in another long full body stretch before getting up. Pulling a robe around her, she went to look for Cowboy.

Her apartment was a small two bedroom on the basement level. Nothing fancy. The front door opened to the living room, which flowed into the kitchen/dining area, and down a hallway to the bedrooms and bathroom. She had decorated the place in what she called thrift store casual. The mismatched couch and chair sat with a three-legged and one cinder block coffee table between them. After she joined Sinister Sisters, Raven had bought a battered shelf unit that she put against the far wall. She stocked it with a small, second hand television she picked up cheap.

She rarely watched it, using it mostly for window dressing, trying to have a normal looking apartment. She had also added some second hand photos that she passed off as family members. The half dozen books were always changing and weren't props. Raven was constantly swapping out her books at the used bookstore.

The rent was cheap because most people don't like the thought of people standing on the sidewalk being able to look down at them through the windows high on the inside wall. Raven used this as an excuse to install permanent thick black-out curtains. All she had to say when someone saw her place for the first time was that she didn't want to become a street side attraction for the degenerates. No one ever questioned her.

Raven slept in the larger bedroom and used the second room as a make-shift music room. It wasn't soundproof, but it was a place she could lay out her music sheets while she wrote lyrics or music. A table, chair, and her acoustic guitar were all she needed. The room was so small it couldn't hold much more than that. When Clarisa and Tina came over to work they used the living room.

She opened the door to the music room and almost hit Cowboy's foot. Everything had been shoved to one side leaving him barely enough room to stretch out on the floor. Good thing sleeping in a coffin-sized space didn't bother him.

Raven poked the bottom of Cowboy's bare foot with her big toe. "Sheriff, hurry, someone's robbing the bank and they've taken the school marm hostage," she said with a twang in her voice.

Cowboy opened one eye, and looked up at her. "You've got the wrong side of the law."

"Oh that's right," said Raven, "you were an outlaw."

"Gunfighter. It was a respectable position," said Cowboy.

"Respectable because no one dared to say otherwise?" said Raven.

"Exactly."

Raven poked his foot with her toe again. "You still drink coffee?"

Cowboy sat up and pulled his feet under him. "Coffee or blood, anything else is a waste of digestive juices."

Raven left Cowboy to get dressed. He'd wanted her to go with him back to the hotel he was staying at. She didn't want to, afraid there would be an expectation of feelings she didn't have for him any more.

Once they had been close. A more primitive time had forced them together. A posse had followed Cowboy all through the night, the full moon giving them enough light to keep following his trail no matter how many times he doubled back or took to the streams. They found his horse's hoof prints and continued to follow.

As the sun began to rise, the posse on his heels, he had stumbled into her cave, faint and weary, in need of nourishment. Raven had been hiding in refuge from some men who saw a native woman as an animal lower than their horses or dogs. A bitch to be used for their own purposes.

Raven still remembered the leader. He was tall with massive shoulders and a muscular body. They had surprised her late at night on the outskirts of a town in Nevada. Raven couldn't recall the name of the town, only that it didn't exist any more. She could recall how easily her fingers dug into the brute's throat as he tried to force himself into her, and the expression on his face as his blood spurted all over her face. She had stopped him, but his men attacked. They tried to kill her. One man roped her from atop his horse and dragged her across the rocky landscape. She had finally gotten her feet under her and was able to jerk the rope, pulling the rider from his horse. She was able to make it to the cave she hid in, but was so weak she was close to death when Cowboy ran in.

When they first looked into each other's eyes, they recognized each other for what they were. Raven had been afraid at first. In her weakened condition she was in no shape to fight a territorial vampire. Before she got a chance to say anything, she heard the sounds of others starting into the narrow entrance of the cave. When the first came into the chamber, Cowboy had grabbed him by his shirt and thrown him against the wall next to where Raven crouched. The stunned man made a slight gurgle as Raven sank her fangs into his throat.

Hot, wet, delicious life flowed from his open throat, into her thirsty mouth. The coppery scent of his blood filled her nostrils, driving her hunger and desire so high it was all she knew. She sucked at his throat like a newborn babe. She sucked, she fed, she lived.

Two vampires in the dark were more than enough for the six men that came to them. Two had torches, and when they came in and saw Raven feasting on their comrade, they froze. Cowboy surprised them from his hiding place and knocked them unconscious before they could fire a shot. It was truly life blood for Raven. They feasted that day, and when the sun set they left together. A bond had formed between them that had them as friends at times, lovers other times, but always someone the other could trust.

The smell of fresh coffee wafted through Raven's apartment. Cowboy came out of the bedroom as if pulled by the scent. He had dressed including his boots. Raven poured them each a mug and they sat at the dinning table.

Cowboy didn't speak until he had taken a sip of his coffee. "I know I don't really need this, but when I was alive this was so much a part of my routine that I haven't been able to give it up."

Raven watched as he blew across the top of the mug before he took another drink.

"What I've been trying to figure out is what you're doing fronting a band when you don't want Demetri to find you," Cowboy said.

"The short version is I got tired of hiding," Raven said. It was her turn to blow on her coffee and drink.

"And tired of living?" asked Cowboy.

Raven shook her head. "No, that's just it. I had been hiding so long in so many places. But I found that I had gotten to a point where I was no longer living, I was merely existing."

"So what did you do?"

"I knew Demetri was sticking to New York, so I came here. They have a great club scene and the Goths here provide enough cover for me to go out. Okay, at first it was fake. I didn't know anyone and hung on the fringes. But to be out with these children. The vibrancy and energy in each one of them. It's like they know they are mortal and shove as much life as possible into their short years."

Cowboy nodded. "Yeah, I've seen that in some too. I'd rather be around them than those normals that spend their lives working and watching television, waiting for retirement so they can start to die."

"Exactly," said Raven, smiling at Cowboy. It felt good to talk to someone who could really understand.

"So what insanity made you jump out of the shadows of the crowd and onto the stage?" Cowboy asked, his tone reprimanding her.

Raven shrugged her shoulders. "It came about from taking the being alive to the next level."

Cowboy shook his head. "Pretend for a moment that I'm still an old cowpoke and haven't taken any philosophy."

"Okay," said Raven. "I was at a club, enjoying the band that was playing. I was singing along with a song I liked. When the song was over these two woman wanted to talk to me. We talked for a bit before they said they had heard me singing and wondered if I was interesting in joining their band."

"So you did."

"Not at first. I turned them down, worried about how easy it would be for Demetri to find me. But then I started to think about it. I mean when you look for a vampire you look in the shadows and alleys, not someone who might be fronting a band."

"The Purloined Letter," said Cowboy.

"What?" asked Raven.

"Hiding in plain site," said Cowboy.

"Right," said Raven as she paused to take another sip of the coffee. "You know how much music has always meant to me. Well, I decided to go for it. I changed my hair yet again and started rehearsing with them."

"That's it?"

Raven looked at Cowboy and then looked away. "Well, they don't know I'm a vampire. They accepted me at face value and we've become friends. I don't know, but there's power in that. No expectations other than we get out there and kick ass on stage and hang out when we're not performing."

Looking at the clock Raven stood. "I've got to get ready for the show tonight."

The ride to the club was quiet. Both of them seemed to be concentrating on the cars and pedestrians around them. Cowboy finally broke the silence.

"Do you think it's safe to continue like this with Demetri actively looking for you all over?"

"He's been looking for me for a long time. Just because a vampire I've never seen before showed up at the club doesn't mean she was working for Demetri. There were a few other vampires there last night. I'll bet they wondered who you were too," said Raven.

"He's expanding his empire, Raven," said Cowboy, his voice showing his exasperation. "He has brought over half of this country under his control. His agents are scouting out the other half, and actively looking for you."

"And how would it look if I took off the night after

this vampire saw me? She'd need to get closer than the shadows of the dance floor to verify who I am. She never did. If she had I would be more worried. The more I think about it the more I think she was just new to the area and enjoying the show. All she did was dance."

"You have to be careful," Cowboy said.

Cowboy's voice had been soft, letting his feelings show. Raven had to remember that he truly cared for her. His motives were not to control her, but to make sure she stayed alive. The rest of the drive went by in silence.

As they walked to the club from where Cowboy had parked his car Raven took his arm in hers and hugged, leaning her head against his shoulder.

"I'll be careful," she said, barely above a whisper.

The club wasn't very crowded when they got there, but it was still early, barely ten o'clock. There was an animated crowd partying in one corner, but Raven didn't even pause. She lead Cowboy back stage

Raven hadn't taken a full step into the storeroom returned-to-dressing room when Tina bounded off her stool and practically jumped into Raven's arms.

"Did you hear? Did you hear?" Tina shouted as she jumped up and down.

"Hear what?" Raven asked. She looked at Clarisa for a clue, but Clarisa only nodded toward Tina, an excited look in her eyes.

"There was a dead body outside in the alley last night," Tina said.

Raven stepped all the way into the room, pulling Cowboy in after her and closing the door. Tina stopped bouncing on her toes.

"Well hello," Tina said.

Raven watched as Tina and Clarisa both let their eyes roam up and down Cowboy's tall frame.

"What's this about a body?" asked Raven.

Tina pouted at her. "What, no introductions?"

Raven sighed. "I'm sorry. This is Lincoln Daynes, an old friend of mine. He's in town on business and looked me up."

Tina stepped closer and shook Cowboy's hand and held it for a couple of seconds longer than normal. "Friend huh, does that mean you're available?"

Clarisa stood up and shook Cowboy's hand too. "Don't mind her, she's not happy if she's not on the make. I for one am glad to know that our girl here isn't a disguised nun."

Raven rolled her eyes and Cowboy gave them a throaty chuckle.

"Ma'am, I'm flattered," Cowboy said as he looked at Tina. "But I'm only in town a few days on business and I'm not the dine and dash sort of guy."

Raven couldn't believe it when Tina actually giggled and blushed.

Cowboy turned to look at both Tina and Clarisa. "I'm pleased to meet you. Raven was telling me what great friends y'all had become. Any friends of hers are friends of mine."

Raven pulled on Cowboy's shoulder. "Whoa there, Cowboy. Better tone it down before that front range folksy charm gets you into trouble."

Everyone smiled, but Raven broke the mood. "Tina, what were you saying about a dead body?"

"Oh! Right. Last night some people found a dead body in the alley after our show."

"Was it anyone we know?" asked Raven.

"No, at least I don't think so," said Tina. "Thing is, these kids from the club found her, and called the police. But before the police got here some guys grabbed the body and took off. When the police got here and there was no body, and they threatened to arrest the guy that called for making prank calls."

"How do you know it wasn't a prank call? Some of the people that come in here are more punker than Goth, and get their jollies doing stuff like that," said Raven.

"Yeah, but there were pictures in the paper," said Tina.

"What? What pictures in what paper?" asked Raven, her head starting to spin with confusion.

Clarisa spoke up. "It seems the cops really pissed off the one's who found the body, so the guy didn't show him the pictures he had taken with his cell phone."

"Yeah, and he took them to a friend and got them in the paper. You know, that one that comes out in the evening," said Tina.

Raven knew she was referring to *Night Life*. It was published in the afternoon and was mostly filled with news and reviews about restaurants, the club scene, and big events.

"Do you have a copy?" she asked Tina.

"No, I saw a copy that some people at the bar were looking at. I think one of the people who found the body was showing it off it his friends."

Raven turned to Cowboy. "Wow, I wonder if that

will bring in more people or keep them away? Lincoln, could you see if you can find a copy while we get ready?"

When the door closed behind Cowboy, Clarisa and Tina started to pepper Raven with questions.

"Where did you meet him? He's a hottie."

"Are you really just friends?"

"Yeah, I'd like to knock boots with that cowboy."

Raven held her hands up in mock surrender. "Guys, guys. I wasn't lying when I said we were old friends. We were more than that once upon a time, but now we're just friends. Come on, I wanted to go over the songs in the first set, to see if you guys think we should move a couple around."

Try as they might to keep talking about Cowboy, Raven resisted, trying to redirect the conversation to other things. Raven wondered why they kept acting like young children when she realized that compared to her they were. When Cowboy returned they had succeeded in accomplishing nothing.

When there was a knock on the door Raven opened it and let Cowboy back in. He had a copy of the paper in his hand. They laid it out on the small makeup table and huddled over it reading the article together. Raven was glad to see it wasn't on the front page.

"Wow," Tina said when they were done reading. "Murder and body snatchers all in one night."

"I don't know, it's a bit scary too," said Raven. She was trying to sound how a human Clarisa's age would sound. "I know I'm going to be careful going home tonight."

Raven looked at the others in the room. She needed

to talk to Cowboy. "We need to go on soon. Do you two think Lincoln and I can have a minute alone?"

Clarisa and Tina both grinned.

"Sure," said Tina.

"Yeah, we'll give you friends some time to, uh, talk," said Clarisa.

Raven heard them giggling in the hall.

"I hope I haven't, as we used to say, sullied your reputation," Cowboy said.

"No, if anything you've enhanced it. Don't worry about them, they're just acting their age. What did you think of the article?"

Cowboy tugged at his lower lip. "Kind of vague. It may have been a prank. The pictures are a little blurry."

"She's the vampire from the audience last night. The one I'd never seen before," said Raven.

"Look at this picture here, on her arm you can see part of a tattoo. Does that look like a crown?" Cowboy asked pointing at one of the pictures.

"Demetri's mark?" Raven said as she leaned closer to the picture, trying to make out more details in the fuzzy image.

"It's hard to tell if it's a tattoo or a piece of trash she is laying on," Raven said.

"But can you take a chance?" Cowboy said.

Raven looked up into Cowboy's eyes. "What chance? This doesn't change anything. We can't tell anything from that picture. And if she is working for Demetri, she was killed right after leaving the club. I doubt she had time to report in."

"But we don't know what she reported before she

came here. We also don't know if she's really dead. According to the article someone grabbed her and hauled her off in a hurry," said Cowboy.

Raven turned away, stepped over the wall and leaned against it. She needed to put some space between her and Cowboy.

"I know you're worried about me, but I don't want to abandon my life that I've got going here on what is right now a vague possibility," Raven said. "I've worked too hard to make friends and establish myself. I'm not going to go back to be a loner in hiding."

"So you're going to go on tonight?"

"I can't see why not," said Raven. She pointed to the paper on the table. "Either she's really alive and will turn up again at the club, or she's dead and I would expect her body to be found after whoever dragged her off is done with her. Either way I'll deal with the milk after it's spilt."

Cowboy spent a couple of minutes looking at his boots. When he looked up at her finally Raven could see the concern in his eyes.

"Let me do this. Let me make a couple of calls to some friends back east. They don't work for Demetri directly, but do a lot of business with his people. I'll give them a story about seeing someone I thought I knew from New York, but couldn't catch up with her. I'll give them a description based on the picture and see if it rings a bell with them."

"But what if they tell Demetri? That might give everything away whether she worked for him or not," said Raven.

"Sweetheart, I've been around long enough to know

74

what to say and what not to say. Trust me, I'll toss in a couple of sexual innuendos, and make up a story about a wild weekend or four, and they won't even think of you. As far as they'll know I'm just looking to get my saddle horn polished."

"Just don't mention my name," said Raven. "Or that you've been to this club or my band."

Cowboy smiled. "That's the old paranoia I've come to expect from you."

"I'm serious. I like my life here and I don't want to give up my freedom because of the grand plans of Demetri. You go make your calls. I'm going to make some music."

CHAPTER SIX

Dafyd Peack shifted the newspapers on his desk around to make room for the garish evening tabloid, *Night Life*. Here and there throughout the newspaper, various headlines had been highlighted in colors corresponding to their import for vampires, and specifically to Dafyd Peack's group. Everything had to be looked over, to be digested, to be filed. Peack's analysts were very good at their jobs.

Green was for good. Yellow meant that it might possibly need to be looked into, but definitely to be filed. Pink was for suspected vampire activity from some local loner vampire. Purple was for something about one of Peack's members, or something related to their businesses—real estate, business, stocks, etc. Orange meant that the article related to other vampire groups.

Dafyd had been seeing too much of this Demetri Vasile lately. Hearing too much about him too. Him and his New York vampire syndicate, and their plans for world domination. Demetri Vasile wasn't the oldest vampire alive, nor was he the first one to try to unite vampires. He wasn't even the only one trying to do that now. Though Dafyd did wonder why some of the other leaders were foolish enough to think that Vasile was some great Washington, or Gandhi, trying to unify a minority for the greater good.

The only good that Demetri Vasile was interested in was his own. It was the one thing you could trust about him.

A fuzzy picture in the evening tabloid was a presumably dead body with Demetri Vasile's tattoo on her arm, the blood-red crown. If Demetri liked to think he was a thoroughly modern vampire, why did he still hold with that ancient prophecy? Did he really think it leant him any legitimacy in his ambitions? Or did he just think to use it before anyone else got the same bright idea?

The paper didn't give the dead woman's name or any other information about her. That didn't mean Dafyd didn't know all of that. He knew she was one of Vasile's spies. His own people had been keeping a watch on her. Her name was Lucrecia Lute. She lived alone in an apartment in one of Vasile's buildings when she wasn't spying. She'd been a vampire for about twenty years, long enough to lose all ties with her normal family, but not so long that she preferred the loner lifestyle. The Goth part wasn't an act, Lucrecia had been into the Goth scene before it was cool.

Most of her business in L.A. had seemed to be scouting out Peack's group. Dafyd felt it was important to keep track of other people's spies, and assumed others did the same with his. He made certain that she didn't really discover the true extent of Peack's Projects, his business front, while ensuring that she thought some ventures were his that really weren't.

That was how the game was played. Dafyd had lived longer than Demetri, and knew that life was a game. A game that could never be won totally, nor lost totally. Nothing ever stayed the same, not the rules, not the players, not the politics, not even the landscape. That's what made the game so fascinating. You never knew what unexpected event would change everything.

And no one lived forever. Not even vampires. There was the illusion of immortality, but the moment you forgot it was only an illusion was the start of your death. Vampires died all the time, by another vampire, a vampire hunter, or even a random fluke accident. Dafyd had seen too many vampire deaths in his time to ever believe in his own invincibility, his own immortality.

Normal human lives might seem like a candle flickering in a strong breeze, easily extinguished, but Dafyd knew that tiny flickering candle could blaze a wildfire no one could tame. For all that they were short-lived, they could still amass more wealth and power than some of the longest-lived vampires.

There was room enough in the world for everyone, normals and vampires, the strong and the weak, cooperatives and loners. You just had to learn how to play the game.

Dafyd sighed, as he looked at the grainy photographs, with their multi-colored dots obscuring as much as they revealed. The paper claimed the woman had been dead, but an unconscious vampire would appear to be dead. The Goths that had found her claimed that some men had taken her away in their van.

He knew that hadn't been his people. Kayze, the woman he'd set to spy over Lucrecia, had reported that she'd left the club with some ignorant yokel, presumably to feed, and Kayze couldn't find them after they'd left. No one had seen Lucrecia after that, except the four Goths.

They knew now, from where the paper said that she'd been found, that she'd taken the far alley away from the club, which strengthened the theory that she'd gone to feed on some fool she'd picked up at the club. Obviously that hadn't gone as planned.

What had happened?

Time to look at this problem from a different standpoint. If Dafyd had sent her out to spy for him, and she disappeared, leaving him with no more information than what was in this lurid excuse for a newspaper, he'd assume some rival organization had snatched her. Presumably to find out what information she knew, and possibly to kill her. Assuming, of course that she wasn't already dead.

If she had been one of his people, he would pull out all the stops to rescue her if she were still alive, or to exact revenge if she wasn't. That would be what his people would expect. That's why they gave him their loyalty.

That was how the game was played.

So Dafyd had to assume that Demetri would do the same.

The problem was that Dafyd didn't have the woman. Hadn't kidnapped the woman. Hadn't killed her. And had no proof of his own, or his people's, innocence.

At a guess, Demetri and his people would descend on L.A. in twenty-four hours or less. They'd take maybe another day to pull information from their spies, determine how to contact Peack's group, and plan their attack.

If Dafyd couldn't produce the woman in less than that time, he'd be facing a war with Demetri.

Well, he'd known he'd have war with Demetri eventually. That was how Demetri operated. The current situation gave Demetri less opportunity to pull any dirty stunts designed to short-cut resistance by killing Dafyd and taking over Dafyd's operations. It put the fight on Dafyd's home turf, which was both good and bad. Good in that it gave Dafyd the advantage. Bad in that whoever and whatever got hurt it would be left to him to clean up. This situation also gave Dafyd the opportunity to short-cut Demetri's plan of attack by finding the woman, with her kidnappers, and delivering them gift-wrapped to Demetri. Which would make Demetri look an idiot for trying to invade Dafyd's territory. And, should anything untoward happen to Demetri during such foolishness, well, that was part of the game, too.

Dafyd pulled his cell phone. "Chuck, assemble the L.A. team and anyone from the New York team that's here. I'll meet you and them in the blue room in twenty minutes. Contact R. and V. in New York, and tell them to get the next flight back. I need them to be here before nightfall, I don't care how they do it, or how much it costs."

He didn't wait to hear Chuck's agreement. These cell phones certainly were an improvement over the old intercom system for the mansion. He sent text messages to the rest of his inner circle. This was one organization that Vasile wouldn't be taking over by cutting off its head. He'd discover three heads taking the place of each one he cut.

Demetri Vasile didn't know enough about Greek mythology, and how it applied to current business practices. Most New Yorkers spent too much time on ancient Chinese military strategy.

After grabbing several paper files, and sending the needed information from his personal computer to the conference computer, Dafyd picked up the tabloid and headed to the blue conference room.

Arriving before anyone else, Dafyd sat at the massive oak desk and powered up the best computer in the house. The room resembled the main parlor of an old-fashioned gentlemen's club. Dafyd had found them perfectly suited to his life when they'd been popular in the Victorian and Edwardian ages, and he learned then that they were without a doubt the best place to conduct business.

Modern conference rooms with large tables ringed with uncomfortable chairs just weren't as good for bringing people around to your way of thinking, nor as good for convincing people that they'd be not only comfortable but genuinely happy doing business with you.

Dark wood paneling set off walls covered in bookcases and showcased the massive fireplace, no fire at this time of year. The large room was liberally strewn with large, well-padded, comfortable chairs and low tables. Modern conveniences such as a large flat screen television connected to the large oak desk's computer, soft indirect lighting from panels above the bookcases, and state of the art fire, earthquake, and burglar alarms had been added for even more convenience.

Before Dafyd had finished assembling his presentation on the computer, Flavian entered.

"There's a problem?"

"A big problem," Dafyd handed the tabloid to him.

Flavian shared the tabloid with Monique, Nguyen, Oscar, Petra, and Gabrielle as they entered.

"I've asked Chuck to assemble the L.A. team here, along with anyone currently in residence from the New York team. I've sent for R. and V. from New York."

"Vasile will be here within twenty-four hours," Petra said, as she took her favorite chair near the fireplace.

"I'll get my team mobilized on finding her and her kidnappers," Nguyen said, as coordinator for the L.A. team. "We'll have them ready to hand them off when Demetri's plane lands."

Dafyd took a moment to reflect that the greatest thing about surrounding yourself with people who were intelligent and powerful in their own right was that you didn't need to tell them what had to be done. The power of democracy was that such people put you in charge, rather than trying to take supremacy away from you.

Chuck and the others began trickling in at that point. Dafyd started the meeting as everyone made themselves comfortable in the cushy chairs. He indicated to Flavian that the tabloid should be passed around.

"If I may draw your attention to the screen." Dafyd waved his hand at the flat screen on the wall. "This is Demetri Vasile. Vampire. Old. Selfish. He has an organization of his own headquartered in New York. He has plans for world domination."

Kayze giggled, and a few others snorted.

"He's deadly serious. With an emphasis on deadly." Dafyd switched to the next image. "Him with a couple of his lieutenants. He runs his organization like a tyranny. He is the tyrant." He ran through a series of photographs of Demetri with his people, in New York, dining, attending a show, walking. "He has absorbed many other groups and operations throughout the United States. We are currently blocking his efforts to take over Chicago. Quietly and behind the scenes so that he doesn't know it is us. His favorite hostile take-over tactic is to assassinate the head of a group, then mop up the ensuing mess." He paused long enough that everyone looked at him. "Note that we can find no vampires living in New York that aren't part of his group. No loners."

Dafyd switched the screen to show a computer–scanned image of the tabloid's photo. "This is Lucrecia Lute. Kayze was following her. She was a spy for Demetri. See the tattoo? It's Demetri's identifying mark. This article, being passed among you, states that she was found dead near the club where she was last seen dancing. According to witnesses she was taken away, dead or unconscious, by a group of men in a van pretending to be police.

"We are assuming that Demetri will think we did this, since he was spying on us for his planned take-over. He should be here with force within a day."

Nguyen stood up from his chair. "My team will be responsible for tracking down these witnesses, then tracking where Lucrecia was taken. We must retrieve her, and capture her kidnappers." He looked at and nodded to the members of his team.

Petra spoke next from her chair. "Everyone else here must be mobilized against the possibility that she isn't found. Watches will be mounted on the airport, this mansion, and all of Peak's Projects public buildings. We'll all be pulling guard duty."

"Should we alert the local loners?" Flavian asked. "We

had planned to do so if we weren't able to stop him east of the Mississippi."

"Not yet," Dafyd said.

"If we can get a license plate number or at least a partial, I know someone at motor vehicles," Monique said.

"The Goths in this article are regulars at the club," Kayze said, as she handed the tabloid over to another member of the L.A. team. "They're probably there now." She stood up. "I'll head out, before this is finished and call if I spot them." She left quickly.

Oscar shifted in his chair causing it to creak. His massive bulk easily dwarfed chairs that swallowed others. "We need more intelligence. I'll get all my team on that. We'll know when Demetri leaves New York, when his plane will land, and we'll search for his worms. There has to be something we can use, if we can't locate his spy."

"The local vampire hunters will be edgy," Gabrielle said. "They may be a problem."

Dafyd turned to Oscar. "Both of you keep an eye on the known hunters. We need to know where they're at and what they're doing."

"They may be responsible for this," Oscar said. "It's possible that a group of hunters picked her up as she was about to feed, hid because the Goths stumbled onto them, then spirited her off to kill somewhere else."

"Assuming that the yokel that left with her wasn't part of an ordinary gang or fraternity that thought it would be entertaining to have a little fun with a helpless Goth," Gabrielle said.

"Speculating isn't going to help us." Dafyd switched the screen to split it between Lucrecia and Demetri. "We need to deal with hard facts, and to do that we need to get hard facts. If we haven't gotten any soon, we'll start speculating."

"Find her, get him," Oscar said.

Dafyd laughed. "That pretty much covers it."

The meeting broke up, everyone leaving to their duties. Dafyd returned to his office to finish sorting through the data on his desk. Every so often someone would call in to report.

"The Goths are at the club, we're interviewing them," Kayze reported. "I've got them convinced I'm with another paper."

"Any license plate numbers?" Dafyd asked.

"Partial. I've already given it to Monique."

Monique called shortly after that. "I've run the partial that Kayze gave me. Do you have any idea how many light colored vans there are in the L.A. metro area? I've got Oscar's people sorting through it to find the most likely. Then we'll start running them down to find the right one."

Oscar arrived in person. The floor creaked as he approached Dafyd's office door, and Dafyd called, "Come in," before Oscar could knock.

"Demetri has been a busy boy. He's sending people to Chicago to upset the balance of power there. But as near as we can tell he doesn't yet know about Lucrecia's disappearance. The major newspapers haven't picked up on it yet."

"I don't suppose we ought to hope he doesn't find out." Dafyd sighed, wishful thinking never worked.

"Those Goths are going to try to get the word out somehow, and twist it around to be some sort of discrimination against one of theirs." Oscar shook his head. "What about Chicago?"

"We can't spare the people now; send our intelligence along to the appropriate parties." Dafyd ran his hand through his hair. "That will have to hold until we can settle our problems here. Any break-through on the partial?"

"None yet." Oscar turned to head toward the door. "Demetri may have to have a fatal accident while he's here."

"That would probably be the best for everyone." Dafyd turned back to his reading. If they didn't find Lucrecia tonight, then tomorrow they would have to meet to brainstorm other solutions.

Flavian called. "None of the loners we've contacted so far knows anything about it. Though a couple of them contacted us, to make sure we'd seen the spread in the paper."

"Basically what we expected." Dafyd sighed.

"Just about every vampire hunting group and fraternity owns a light colored van. We've got the youngsters circulating through the colleges, especially the frat houses, checking for any rumors that might help. Still trying to figure out how we could get someone undercover into a vampire hunting group." Flavian sounded tired. "We didn't want to wait until the plates came through, just in case. It's not a very likely scenario, but it is possible."

"Has anyone seen anything on this yokel she was going to feed on?" Dafyd asked.

"Not that I've heard about."

"I think he may be key to the whole thing. We need to

find him too. If she did feed on him there either should have been a body, or some blood, or some indication that he got away." Dafyd stared at the picture in the paper.

"From what Kayze said, he was apparently a Goth wanna be, and no one at the club recognized him."

"Find him. He's key to finding Lucrecia."

After that it was silent in Dafyd's office for far too long.

The next call was from Gabrielle. "It's getting too close to dawn. I'm calling my people in. You'd better have all the others called in too. We'll have to mount watches through the day, but there's nothing more we can do at this point."

Dafyd nodded to himself. Gabrielle was right. Now was the time to regroup, and rethink their options.

He sent the message for everyone to come in. Then he started preparing for a much bigger meeting in the main parlor. Everyone needed to be there for this meeting. They'd need as much input as possible, and everyone had to know what everyone else had done and would be doing. This was too important to pretend it wasn't happening.

Keeping his people informed and on track was vital. Letting everyone know they were an important part of the group kept them loyal. They all had to be in on this.

That was how Dafyd played the game.

It looked like the game they were going to play was war.

CHAPTER SEVEN

During the first set, Raven kept looking into the audience for signs of unknown vampires, or worse, Demetri. It didn't help that the article in the newspaper had brought out a larger than normal audience. With so many people Raven had never seen before filling the room in front of the stage, she was constantly spinning to look at someone with the pallor of death on their face. It was the first time she ever saw a disadvantage of hanging out with people who either by choice of makeup or lifestyle had the pigmentation of a corpse.

"You're really working the crowd tonight, Raven," Tina said during their break.

"Seriously," said Clarisa. "You're all over the stage and making eye contact. You'd think there was someone from a label out there tonight."

Raven smiled and shrugged her shoulders. "You never know. There's just so many people I've never seen before I guess I'm really pumped up."

"Yeah, I know what you mean. It feels like there's a lot of energy in the room," Tina said.

"And we're rocking the house," said Clarisa. "Did you see how they reacted to the set?"

Wanting to continue pushing the conversation away from herself, Raven said, "And Charlie can't complain either. There were so many people lined up for drinks at the end of the set I saw him go behind the bar to help."

Tina added a couple of dabs to her makeup while Clarisa and Raven finished changing their clothes. When they left for the second set, Raven checked outside the door and down the hall before stepping out. She was out of practice for checking for the unexpected, but was forcing herself to readjust.

Raven knew she was walking a fine line. She didn't want to give up her current life, but that meant she had to continue like there was nothing wrong. It wasn't like she could turn to Tina and Clarisa and say, "Oh, by the way I'm a 400-year-old vampire and another vampire is trying to find me so he can rule over me. He might even kill me." No, if she wanted to keep her friends she was going to have to keep them in the dark and act as normal as possible.

The second set went even better than the first. The audience gave off a charged vibration that fed the band and pushed them to perform better. The more intense the performance, the higher the audience got. It was a feedback loop of the greatest high, and Raven couldn't deny that it gave her a rush.

Raven let her body go with the flow of the music and threw herself around the stage in rhythmic flings that reminded her of her normal youth so long ago among her tribe during the great celebrations of life. It also gave her an opportunity to continue watching the entire audience for signs of enemies.

When they finished the set there was such a steady applause they actually had to perform an encore. It was a first, but they had plenty of material and the three ripped out two more songs before calling it a night. Raven could see that Tina and Clarisa were on an adrenaline high, it showed in their eyes though they were tired.

"It's almost a let down, you know," said Tina. "I mean I think that was our best show ever, and now its over and we have to be ordinary again."

Clarisa picked up two of the cases and headed to the back. "Yeah, it's almost like a drug. That was so mind blowing of a show that I want it again and again."

"No arguments here," said Raven as she hoisted her guitar and amp backstage. "I do think we've set the high mark for us to try for every night."

"All we need is to get the same audience," said Clarisa.

"I don't know. Maybe because we've been playing to a lot of regulars we've gotten a bit stale," said Raven.

The last of the equipment was stored and the three started for the front of the club. "Kind of like sex," said Tina.

"Excuse me?" said Raven.

"You know, like when you've been with the same guy a while and sex gets to be the same all the time. Push here, rub there, wheeeeeeee, everybody scream," Tina said while making hand motions in the air in front of her to go with the directions she was giving.

Clarisa laughed. "Girl, I think you've got the start of a new song."

"Stale Sex by Sinister Sisters," said Tina. "Yeah, I could see that on a CD."

When they stepped out front the crowd paused their conversations, drinking, and dancing to the canned music. More applause and Raven could swear Clarisa was blushing. A few people came over and started talking to them, telling them how great the show had been. A couple were regulars, but most were new to the club.

Raven tried to join in the laughter. She responded to the compliments automatically, her eyes again worked to pierce the low lighting and see everyone in the room. She was becoming concerned because Cowboy hadn't come back yet. Offers of free drinks drew them over to the bar.

"Hey Charlie, have you seen my friend that was here earlier? Tall, dark and cowboy boots," said Raven.

Charlie looked up at her, a glazed look in his eyes. His hair was in need of some serious mirror time and sweat lines could be seen on the sides of his face where drops of sweat had rolled down from his hair. He seemed to be having trouble focusing on her.

"Raven," Charlie said.

"Yeah. Have you seen my friend?"

Charlie shook his head. "I've been running my ass off back here. I haven't seen anyone who wasn't ordering a drink for the last two hours."

Charlie normally sat in his office or walked around the back of the club. The large crowd was making him work.

"Sorry to hear you're having a bad night," Raven said.

"Bad night? This is a great night," said Charlie. "What got into you guys tonight? This crowd is fantastic. And more are sticking around after the live show is over. Can you do it again?"

"We'll do our best," Raven said.

She turned back and found Tina and Clarisa sitting at a table with some others. Tina caught her eye and waved her over, pointing to an empty chair next to her. Raven saw a glass of beer was waiting in front of her as she sat. She sipped it out of politeness but couldn't help think of how unlike blood it tasted.

Unfortunately, Tina had given her a chair so Raven had her back to the door. She kept twisting around to see who was coming into the club.

"He'll be back," said Clarisa from her chair across the table.

"What?" Raven asked.

"Sweetie, you've been spinning in that chair more than my ADHD kid brother. Lincoln will be back. He's a fool if he doesn't."

It wasn't just Cowboy that had Raven keeping an eye on the door. Since she couldn't explain the others she wanted to see before they saw her, she let it go. "Sorry, I didn't mean to be rude."

"I'd be willing to be rude for a hunk like him," said Tina.

"I've seen the guys you date and it wouldn't take someone as good looking as that to give you a rude 'tude," said Clarisa.

Raven couldn't help but laugh at Tina's mock expression of shock.

"Relax, Raven," said Clarisa. "I'll keep my eyes open

and let you know when he gets here."

"Thanks, my neck was beginning to get a little sore," Raven said. She was able to stop her urges to constantly look over her shoulder, but felt like the hairs on the back of her neck were constantly standing at attention.

Two hours later, Raven was starting to get worried. No matter how much she tried to console herself with the knowledge that Cowboy had stayed alive for centuries and in some areas more savage than the LA night scene, she couldn't help but keep picturing him lying in a heap like the photographs of the waif girl vampire from the previous night.

Clarisa had said her goodnights from the arm of a rather handsome tall redheaded man who looked good in his tight black jeans. Now Tina was waving goodbye from the doorway. Raven smiled and waved back as Tina hooked her arms into those of the two men seeing her home. "Brothers," Raven thought she heard Tina giggle as she headed for the door.

Raven wasn't sure what to do. She had politely turned down similar offers that Tina and Clarisa had taken. She had hoped that Cowboy would come back to the club so she could find out what he learned, and give her a ride home. The buses had stopped running hours before, and there was no way in hell she would be able to get a cab at this time of night in this neighborhood.

Resolving herself to have to make the three-mile walk home, Raven left a couple of hours before dawn. The outside air was cooler than the recycled body heated air of the club. She breathed deep, filling her nostrils with the scents of the street. The smell from the hint of humidity was nice, but didn't mask the odors of rotting food from the dumpsters in the alley. Raven didn't need further prodding to start walking home. She moved quickly, but kept to the shadows.

The neighborhood around the club still had some activity as people headed home from the bars and dance clubs that were in the area. All-night diners did a brisk business in the early morning hours, too. A few blocks from the club the streets became more residential, the only businesses were those of the nine to five variety. As she walked, Raven started to feel that someone was following her.

She had been keeping a lookout as she passed streets, alleys, and other dark recesses. She hadn't seen anyone, but now she could hear what sounded like the faint sound of someone walking behind her. At first she thought it was an echo of some sort of her own footsteps. She changed her pace to a little faster and then a little slower. It wasn't her, someone was following her.

She tried looking into the side mirrors of cars parked along the curb to see if she could see who was behind her, but she could never get the angle right. She didn't want to alert whoever it was that she knew they were there. If it was one of Demetri's people she wanted to capture them for information. If it was a hunter, well that was a case of getting them before they got her. It was times like this Raven wished she had Hollywood vampire powers. It would be nice to change to a bat and fly home.

A few feet before the next corner Raven started to

run and went around the corner. She stopped when she had rounded the corner and pushed her back against the wall of the building and waited. A man came running around the corner a few seconds later. Raven reached out after he passed her and grabbed the back of his collar. The man made a gagging gurgling sound as his own shirt choked him. His momentum stopped by Raven's superior strength threw him off balance and he fell to the sidewalk.

Raven was on him before he could recover. She sat on his stomach with her feet hooked back over his legs. Her hands held his wrists over his head and she leaned over, her face inches from his. She could feel his pulse fluttering under hands in his wrists, feel the beat of his heart race faster. Sense the flow of the blood through his body. She could see fear in his eyes.

"Who are you?" she asked, her tone low and her voice filled with menace.

The man under her thrashed about wildly, trying to free himself. His head wagged back and forth, not looking up at her.

"Lemme go. I wasn't doin' nothin'," said the man as he continued to squirm.

Raven applied pressure to his arms and legs with her body. "Who are you? What do you want with me?"

"Nothin'. Let me up. You're crazy, lady," he said.

"Then why were you following me? Why did you chase me around the corner? Who are you working for?" Raven flicked the left wrist in her hand and heard the bone snap.

The man screamed in pain. He writhed under her, his blood rushing through his body, driven faster by his fear. It was calling to her. When his cries had died down to whimpering, Raven asked him again, "Why were you following me?"

"Okay, okay," the man said, "please don't hurt me. I was following you to mug you. You were alone and the way you kept looking all around you looked like an easy target."

"But I'm not," said Raven, feeling the fire of the hunt flowing through her body. "Can you give me a reason why I shouldn't kill you here and stop you from hurting others?"

The man's whimpering got louder and his face screwed into a grimace. He started to cry. "Please don't. I'm sorry. I won't do it again. Please don't kill me."

"But I'm hungry," said Raven, showing her fangs to the hunter turned prey.

His eyes got wider than Raven thought possible. He thrashed about, shaking his head back and forth. He kept repeating himself, begging her to leave him alone. This wasn't an operative for anyone, just a petty thief. Raven grabbed his hair in her fist and jerked his head to one side. She held it there as she bent over him, gagging his screams with her shoulder. She felt him thrash harder when he felt her breath on his neck.

Raven savored the moment. The feeling of control. The anticipation of blood, hot and pumping from a human heart. Her mouth watered with her own desire and she sunk her fangs into the mugger's throat.

Blood gushed from the wound, rushing into her mouth, rolling across her tongue and down her throat. The taste, so hot, tangy, a rich taste that was never as good from siphoned and bagged blood. Raven drank, her provider having fainted beneath her. She took enough to sate her hunger for a few weeks, but not enough to kill him, or even turn him into one of her kind. He was not worthy, and Raven never brought scum over from the norms.

Raven doubted he would be attacking anyone else soon. She pushed herself off his stomach. In fact he would probably have a lot more respect for women and find himself a new line of work. Raven looked down at the unconscious man lying on his back. A trickle of blood dripped to the sidewalk, it would already be clotting. Raven saw that he had wet his pants.

The rest of her walk was uneventful, for which Raven was grateful. She got home about an hour before dawn, but was disappointed to not find Cowboy waiting for her. She realized that she didn't know what hotel he had been staying at, or any way to get a hold of him.

A few minutes before the sun was due to rise there was a knock on the door. Raven had worked herself into a state of agitated worry that she flung the door open without looking through the peephole first. Cowboy was standing on the other side. He wasn't wounded or disheveled as if he had been in a fight. He wasn't a captive of Demetri, being forced to reveal where she was. He hadn't experienced any of the horrible fates Raven had been imagining for most of the night.

"Where the hell have you been?" Raven shouted at him.

"Uh, hello to you too," Cowboy said, a confused look on his face.

"Well?" Raven said. She was letting all of the pent

up fear and frustration flow out of her. Her body shaking, muscles taunt, ready for anything.

"Perhaps I can come in so your neighbors can sleep," Cowboy said.

Raven realized that she was standing in doorway, shouting at him. Stepping back allowed Cowboy to step in, and Raven closed the door behind him.

"So, where were you? I've been worried to death about what happened to you. I thought maybe you had met up with whoever had killed that vampire last night," Raven said, her arms crossed in front of her chest.

Cowboy stepped away from her and sat on the couch. "What's wrong? I told you I'd see you later. I had to make a couple of phone calls and then I had to go to work."

"You never said anything about going to work," Raven said. "I waited around the club for you, worried sick when you didn't come back."

Cowboy got up and walked over to her. He put his hands on her shoulders. "I'm sorry you were worried, but I still have work to do too. I had to do the final inspection on the installation my team just finished up, and there were some adjustments I had to personally take care of. Then my customer wanted to talk to me about some other ideas, a larger version of my rooms. He's a major player in this town so I couldn't exactly blow him off."

Raven let Cowboy pull her into his arms. She didn't want to be angry, but couldn't let it go. She could smell his skin, the mix of soap from hours ago under the more recent sawdust and oils. As he held her he began to sway with her in his arms. Raven felt her muscles relax. It had been a long night of highs and lows.

Raven gave Cowboy the short version of her night. The night playing music, the creepy feeling sitting with her back to the door hoping he would come back, and her run in on the way home.

"I didn't mean to worry you. If you had a phone," Cowboy let his voice trail off, his sentence unfinished.

Raven shrugged. "You're right. It's one of my strategies to stay off the Demetri's radar. It's amazing what people can find out about someone else on the internet with little more than a name or phone number."

"You should try one of the new prepaid cell phones," Cowboy said. He kissed her forehead and his arms released her from his embrace. "You can have a number, friends can call you, and you don't have to have your real name for anyone to find. Coffee?"

They moved into the kitchen. Raven put a fresh filter into the pot before measuring scoops of ground coffee into it. After she had added the water she turned back to Cowboy.

"Did you make your calls, Mr. Phone Expert?" she asked, letting a smile play across her lips.

Cowboy picked up the mugs they had left in the drainer the previous morning and set them down next to the coffee maker that was dripping coffee into the glass carafe. "Yes, but I wasn't able to get too much information."

"What did you find out?" Raven asked.

"I called a couple of friends to just chat, you know, tell them how screwed up it is out here and how I can't wait to get home," said Cowboy.

Raven poured them both a cup of coffee.

"And?"

"Well, I told them that I saw a cute looking vampire at a club that looked familiar, but I couldn't place her. I thought that she might be from New York too. I described what she looked like based on the picture in the paper."

"Did anyone know her?" asked Raven.

"The first two, no," said Cowboy. He blew steam from the top of his mug and took a sip. "But the third guy I talked to said she sounded like someone he's seen around the clubs in Manhattan. Her name is Lucrecia or Lucinda or something like that."

Raven studied her coffee for a minute. "How sure was he? I mean it was just a description."

"He knew about her tattoo. The woman he was thinking of works for Demetri. She's one of his operatives that scopes out new territories. He doesn't see her for weeks at a time, and then she's back at the clubs."

"Let me guess. He hasn't seen her in a while," said Raven.

"Not for at least a week," Cowboy said.

Raven walked back into the living room. She sat on the couch and sipped her coffee. Cowboy followed her and sat on the other end of the couch. They turned toward each other.

"Did he know if Demetri knew anything?" Raven asked.

"I'm sorry," said Cowboy. "This was one of the guys

that works for me. I have him in New York putting in systems. Since he doesn't work for Demetri he has no idea."

Raven took another sip of her coffee. "So we are pretty sure the vampire found in the alley worked for Demetri. What we don't know is why she was here. If she regularly goes into new territories for him and likes the club scene, her being at the club last night may have been a coincidence."

"That's a mighty tall coincidence," said Cowboy.

"True," said Raven. "And whether by coincidence or if she was specifically there because of me, we don't know if she passed anything on to Demetri."

"A lot of open questions. You know this town better than I do. Any ideas where you might be able to find some information?" said Cowboy.

"I think," said Raven, "that I'm going to have to do what my people have always done when they needed answers they couldn't find within themselves."

Raven looked up at Cowboy and saw his perplexed expression.

"Tonight we're going to go see The Shaman," said Raven.

CHAPTER EIGHT

Because of the wildly spectacular test of Matt's new machine, none of Vic's group had gone out to do any real vampire hunting. Instead, they'd divided themselves into three groups.

One group with Vic and Matt and Ekson spent their time pouring over the data from the night of the kill. A second group spent most of their time running errands, finding more equipment for the improved version, doing whatever was necessary to obtain whatever Vic and Matt required. Truck, Stevo, Ken, and Pete were in that group.

Jim found himself in the third group with Mike, Lewis, and Woo. They spent their time hunting, but only to reconnoiter. They didn't kill any vampires they found. What they were doing was tracking down rumors of vampire gathering places.

Vic had always cautioned everyone to avoid such places before. The strength and speed of one vampire made it very difficult to overpower and kill unless the numbers were in the hunters' favor. The vampire hunters had always figured that a group of vampires was best left alone. They fought by isolating a vampire then killing it.

As a group the vampire hunters were more effective and more efficient, but it made for slow going. They averaged about two vampires a week. Which was more than any one of them could have done, but to Jim it still felt slow. He wanted them dead. All of them dead. Now.

He wasn't alone with that wish.

The thought of being able to take out a whole group of vampires had energized the previously enervated group. Everyone was charged and up. Everyone wanted to do anything to see this happen, like making this new improved machine work.

There were a few problems though.

"But won't people notice a building missing the next day?" Mike asked. "Except for the melted metal left on the pavement where it used to be?"

"I don't care what happens to the mansion," Lewis said, looking back from where he sat shotgun in the group's van. "As long as the vampires are gone."

"Think about it." Mike turned to Jim, possibly hoping for someone else to be practical. "I mean if this mansion we're scoping out turns out to be full of vampires, and we *do* find some way of putting the mirrors all around, and the new machine works as well as that demo, then won't people notice the next morning when the mansion is gone?"

"I'm sure they've thought of that." Woo turned the wheel to the left, following whatever directions Lewis gave him. "That's their problem. Ours is finding a location filled with vampires."

"What if the place is a mixture of vampires and normal people?" Jim asked.

"I suppose that depends," Lewis said, looking up from the map in his lap. "If there are too many innocents then we'll have to find another location."

"And how many is too many?" Mike asked.

"I don't know," Lewis said.

"It also depends on if they're really innocents, or if they're vampire sympathizers." Woo sounded contemptuous. "They may be ordinary people, but if they're those idiots that are feeders for the vamps or helping them out somehow, then everyone'd be better off without them."

"Still, how many is too many?" Mike asked.

"One," Jim said. "One is too many."

"Even if they're sympathizers?" Woo asked.

"I don't know," Jim said. "I've never killed a sympathizer."

"I have." Woo took a corner just a little too fast. "Better to kill one of them than to let them lure you to their 'master.'"

"You make it sound like an old black-and-white movie," Mike laughed. "Renfield or Igor slobbering around." He started doing a raspy-voiced movie imitation. "Yes, master. You must feed. But, no master, I don't know the difference between the beautiful woman in the flimsy nightdress and the nasty vampire hunter with a wooden crossbow bolt." He shook his head. "All because the plot required it. No wonder they were generally lousy movies."

Woo snorted. "The sympathizers are basically vampire wanna-bes. They hang out with them hoping one of the vampires will make a vampire out of them. As far as I'm concerned they're all the same."

"Do all of them know they're hanging out with vampires?" Jim asked.

"How could they not notice?" Lewis asked. "You'd think the night-life, no sunlight, cold skin, no sweating, fangs, and weird eating habits would clue them in."

Jim thought about his sister. Tracey had been so naïve. She just wanted the thrill of dating a bad boy. Well, he'd been a bad boy all right. Jim wasn't sure he could assume that all the vampire sympathizers did know they were vampire sympathizers. Some might just be too stupid and trusting, or unbelievers.

"We're still left with the problem of the mansion and all its furnishings," Mike said, returning to his favorite topic.

"Oh, give it a rest." Woo pulled the van to the curb. "You two walk from here. Got your case?"

Mike and Lewis each pulled a plain black messenger case. They were disguised as salesmen. Jim and Woo would be in the van, sitting or cruising around, trying to listen in with their spying devices and checking out anyone on foot in the neighborhood.

"Our target is over there." Woo nodded toward a mansion that could have been the high-class older brother of Vic's mansion.

A Victorian, older but in much better condition than Vic's, restored and cared for, but sitting in a neighborhood that was still in the process of renovation. Some of the neighboring houses had been subdivided into three, four, and five apartments. A few were mixed business and residential. Some were commercial, housing stores, medical offices, and the like.

The house that they parked in front of housed a new-age Wiccan shop, a dentist, and one empty office.

Jim had no idea what sort of salesmen Mike and Lewis were supposed to be. He didn't want to pry, but he wasn't sure what they were going to do if someone did want to buy something.

They'd decided not to either start or finish at the target mansion. They didn't want to appear to be bogus. So they were going to knock on just about every door in the neighborhood.

Woo and Jim sat in the middle and back of the van, where the tinted windows made it hard for anyone to see in. A simple cheesecloth curtain pulled across the backs of the front seats insured that no one could see in from the front. They didn't want to be spied on while they were spying.

"Let's keep the chit-chat to a minimum," Woo said.

Jim nodded. They might not be the only ones with listening equipment. "Give me a sign if you get anything important."

Nodding, Woo said, "I'll take left, you take right."

Grimacing Jim nodded. Of course Woo would choose the side with their target mansion. "We probably ought to switch later."

Woo frowned, but nodded.

Jim started concentrating his efforts on the wrong side of the street. Listening in on what was happening in the building. His finger hovered over the button that would start the recording equipment, but he didn't want to waste space recording the dentist's drill from up over the Wiccan shop.

From the sound of the drill, someone had been putting off their visit to the dentist for far too long.

"So as I was saying," a man said over the sound of the drill. "We're looking for a new place, the old owner sold this place, and the new one says that as soon as this contract is up he is raising the rent. We'll send you a postcard as soon as we know the new address."

"Think they'll get rid of that cult across the street?" a woman asked.

Jim raised his eyebrows as he hit the record button. Maybe he shouldn't underestimate dentists; like lawyers they were one of the most hated professions.

"I think the cult across the street is the landlord," the man said. "Hand me the probe. Or at least the leader of the cult is the owner. They seem to be buying up most of the street. Perhaps they're getting more followers."

After that they seemed more interested in talking about the dental procedure at hand or last night's game. Jim turned off the record, but kept listening, just in case they made some other remark that might be pertinent.

He couldn't help thinking about what he'd heard as he waited for something useful. What use did vampires have for mansions and property? Obviously they had to have somewhere to live, but beyond that, why buy up a neighborhood? What would be the purpose?

In the searching the four of them had done so far, they hadn't found one vampire club or vampire hangout. Any number of places had rumors about them, but not one had proved true. The vast majority of vampires Jim had run into were loners. Most of the ones the vampire hunters caught were loners.

Maybe, Jim thought, they didn't find many places where vampires congregated because vampires didn't congregate. But if vampires didn't congregate then the new machine would be useless.

Giving up on the boring dentist and his shrill drill, Jim checked the empty office. He heard nothing. He turned the pick-up toward the Wiccan shop. He heard Celtic music, that he didn't record, and that probably shouldn't have been recorded for the store in the first place.

He moved the pick-up again, to the next house.

Why would vampires acquire property?

Why did anyone acquire property?

Money and power. But, what use did vampires have for money or power? They didn't need much. Didn't have to eat. Just needed shelter during the day away from the sun. Any basement would do. Clothing and other accessories they could acquire from whoever they fed off. They had no family, or most didn't. Most didn't even have jobs, or obligations. They were undead.

Money and power were needed for domination.

Jim gasped. Did the undead want domination? Over the living?

Woo looked up. "What did you get?"

"They're buying up the neighborhood," Jim whispered. "Do you think they're looking to acquire power? To take us over?"

"You are such an idiot." Woo readjusted his equipment. "What else would they be doing?"

"But they're loners," Jim hissed.

"Some of them yes," Woo said. "Remember you're not in Kansas anymore, Dorothy. They also form syndicates and other organizations."

"But what about us?" Jim asked.

"What about us?" Woo said.

"Are there other groups like us? Organizations? Syndicates?"

"Yes." Woo tapped his headphones. "Listen now. Talk later."

Jim returned to his equipment. He'd never met any other vampire hunters until he'd met Vic's group one night. They'd been unknowingly stalking the same vampire. After Jim had staked him, he'd turned around to find several men watching him.

He ran, afraid they'd turn him in to the police. Luckily they'd caught him. Thanked him. Told him they too were vampire hunters.

That had been a shock. Most people didn't even seem to believe in vampires. He'd been so surprised, so glad, so relieved, to find others like himself; he'd never thought much about it since.

If vampire hunters could organize, so could vampires. Jim felt like an idiot for not thinking of it. He wondered what else he hadn't thought about. He'd have to find some time later to think for a bit.

Training his pick up on the Wiccan shop, Jim returned to listening dutifully. The shop now had someone in it. Neither they nor the shopkeeper seemed particularly bright. They were worrying over some foot problem and what herbs could be used to cure it.

Jim looked over at Woo, who was intently recording something. Trust Woo to get all the good stuff. To make Jim look even more like a stupid hick. He thought about Woo's comments. Did the others think he was just some stupid idiot?

Then, the conversation in the shop took an interesting turn. The customer, a woman, was now asking the shopkeeper, also a woman, about an aphrodisiac. Jim barely stopped himself before he snorted. He might not be the brightest bulb in the box, but he knew enough to realize that there was no such thing as an aphrodisiac. Still the woman behind the counter seemed more than willing to sell any of several options to the customer.

When the woman left the shop, Jim flinched in sympathy for whoever her target was. The aphrodisiac the woman needed was to acquire some style and stop looking like a lamppost.

"There's nothing more here," Jim whispered to Woo. "I think we'd better cruise."

Woo gave him the wait-a-minute signal. Jim looked up and down the street. The ugly woman was just emerging from another shop. If it had been night, Jim might have gotten out to talk to her, but they were doing the preliminary search during the day. So no vampires would be out and about now. He didn't even need to check.

Finally Woo put his equipment down. "All right. You check and I'll drive. I'll go slow. If you get anything promising, let me know and I'll stop for a bit."

They drove slowly around the block, three times. Nothing. They parked in the same spot they had vacated earlier.

"What did you get the last time?" Jim asked.

"Snores," Woo said.

Since they'd switched sides, Jim was able to confirm this for himself. The only sound in their target mansion was snores. Not very exciting.

Woo seemed to be having as much success with the other side of the street.

Mike and Lewis returned shortly after that.

"Any luck with the target?" Woo asked.

"None," said Mike.

"No one answered to my knock," said Lewis. "Think it's a bust?"

"Don't know." Woo started up the car and pulled into traffic. "Most of what I got was snores."

"The whole household sleeps during the day?" Mike asked.

"I tried to separate them out. I think there were four snores. What are the chances that everyone works nights in the same household?" Woo asked.

"The dentist said it was a cult," Jim said.

"What?" Woo asked.

"I assume it was the dentist. He was talking over the drill, usually that's not the patient."

"And what exactly did this dentist say?" Mike asked.

Both Mike and Lewis were staring at Jim. A glance in the rear view mirror showed that Woo was trying to look at Jim too.

"Well," Jim said leaning back into the van's bench seat. "The dentist said that the rent was going up and that he thought his building had been bought by the cult across the street, or at least the leader of the cult."

"Did he say anything else, about this cult?" Woo asked.

"No. I can play what I recorded." Jim hit the playback on his equipment. The shrill whine of the drill filled the van, but the dentist's voice came through loud and clear. Must've been all those years of talking over the drill.

"More followers, eh?" said Lewis.

"I think we'd better come back here tonight," Mike said.

"Oh yes." Woo floored it to run a yellow light. "Definitely."

The street looked pretty much the same at night as it had during the day. The shops and offices were all closed, but a few restaurants were open. Yet, there seemed to be as much foot traffic as during the day.

In their target mansion every window was lit up, and people were moving around inside.

"Okay, Jim and Woo, your turn," Mike said. Mike and Lewis settled themselves with the listening equipment.

Jim started walking the street. Trying to look like a tourist. Fearing that he was succeeding all to well.

"Excuse me, but I'm lost," Jim said, stopping the first person he came to on the sidewalk in front of the Wiccan shop. He gave them a bogus address as the place he was looking for. It gave him a chance to examine the man in the light from the closed sign on the store, while the man tried to think of an answer.

The tells were all there, pale skin, a hint of fang around the lips, no visible pulse on his neck.

"Oh, well," Jim said after the man explained he didn't know where that address was. "Do you know any good Chinese places around here?"

"No, sorry," the presumed vampire said.

Jim moved on. Using the same story with each encounter. After the seventh try, Jim started feeling the hair on the back of his neck stand up. Five of the seven were vampires, and he was out here without a stake.

He looked around, and caught a glimpse of two of his questionees pretending not to follow him.

Another quick glance located Woo across the street, talking to some woman. Just down by the next place another woman watched him. Either they were being too obvious, or something was up.

Jim questioned a few more people, without losing his tail. He began to be real nervous when he realized how far he'd gotten from the van. He hurried back, walking right past the two men tailing him. They followed.

He jaywalked across the street to Woo in the middle of the block, noticing that the woman that had been watching Woo earlier was hanging nearby.

"I see you're popular with the ladies," Jim said, trying not to sound nervous.

"Yeah. You appear to be popular too," Woo said, breathlessly.

Wondering why it was that Woo's nervousness made him feel better, Jim said, "Let's get out of here."

They headed for the van.

Once inside, Jim saw his two tails duck into the shadow beside the Wiccan store. Woo looked apprehensively out of the windows, and asked, "You guys ready to go?"

"Not yet. What're you doing back so early?" Mike asked.

"The place is crawling," Woo said, shuddering. "It's almost wall-to-wall out there." He slid into the driver's seat. "I'll pull onto the next street. You can listen from behind the house."

Mike nodded. He looked to Jim. "Is it really that bad?"

Jim tried to smooth the hair down on the back of his neck. "It's bad."

Lewis looked up from what he was recording. "We've hit pay dirt here."

As Woo drove slowly down the street, Mike trained his pick up onto the target mansion.

They sat quietly in the van for over an hour after Woo parked it around behind the mansion. Mike and Lewis kept their equipment trained on conversations in the house.

As time went by Jim saw the blood drain from Mike's face, leaving him almost as pale as a vampire.

"This is not just pay dirt," Mike said. "This is the mother lode."

"I say we get out of here," Lewis said.

It was quiet inside the van for a few minutes as they drove through the night black streets.

"What did you hear?" Jim asked.

At first no one answered him. After taking a deep

breath, Mike said, "That entire mansion is filled with vampires. I think their leader is named Dafyd. And I think they're planning some sort of war."

CHAPTER NINE

Demetri stood in front of the large picture window looking over the city as the horizon started to turn pink. He stepped back from the window and pressed the remote on his desk. Shutters rolled down over the windows from the outside and long thick, black curtains slid across the windows on the inside. Either would have been sufficient to block out the rays of the sun on their own, but Demetri didn't get to where he was by not having back-up plans.

Demetri enjoyed living at the top of a New York skyscraper and the power it gave him—the power in the perception of the other vampires in the city. They could look up at night and see his tower of windows. The message of no fear was there and Demetri used it to his advantage. During the day there were no living vampires to see the shades providing protection, and that was never spoken of.

Demetri noticed that Richard stood in the doorway. "Everyone in?" he asked.

"Yes, everyone is in and working on their reports. You have no meetings scheduled with norms today so we are locked down for the day," said Richard.

Demetri went behind his desk and sat in his leather chair. "Any red flags popping up?"

Richard stepped into the room and sat in one of the chairs in front of the desk. He shook his head. "No, just routine stuff. You can have some downtime if you want."

Demetri chuckled. "I don't think I know what that is any more. I barely get any rest, and if I didn't have blood brought to me I don't know how I'd feed."

"Oh, I'm sure you'd find a way," Richard said.

"Yes. And there are days that I miss the old days. The hunt, the capture, the feeding. It was so primal and could be intoxicating," said Demetri as he looked into the past over Richard's head.

Richard nodded, "Yes, it is very exhilarating. But I spent too many times being the hunted. I don't mind feeding in civilized ways."

"There is that," said Demetri. "It's like when the norms wish for the good old days their ancestors lived in, until they remember that not everyone had flush toilets."

"I know I don't miss that stench," said Richard.

Demetri chuckled at the thought, then shook it off. He had to focus on his plans. "So, do you think young Adam has any results from his searches?"

"He's been hunched over his computer since he left the meeting. I heard him saying something about too many hits so he's probably trying to refine the search. After all, there are a lot of unexplained deaths over a couple of decades that can pop up."

"Well, it gives him a chance to get back in my good graces," Demetri said. "He's a pup and thinks he is truly immortal. He forgets we can be killed and need to take steps to see that we don't."

"He was a young human and is an even younger vampire," said Richard. "He'll learn as he goes. He just doesn't understand why you need Khalida so bad."

"Sometimes I don't think anyone does, even though I explain it over and over," said Demetri. "She is my oldest. I need her by my side."

Demetri looked at Richard who said nothing, but had the look of one who had something to say.

"What," Demetri said.

"No one has said anything, but some of us remember the prophecy," said Richard.

Demetri collected his thoughts before he spoke. He needed the support of his staff, but wasn't sure how vulnerable to appear to them.

"It all adds up to the same thing," Demetri said. "I haven't said anything because we have several youngsters among us. It takes a couple of centuries for one of our kind to get a true eternal perspective and appreciate the existence of things that can't be explained."

"So how does it add up? I've been around awhile, I think I can take it," said Richard.

"Okay, but for now I don't want this to leave this room."

Richard nodded his agreement.

"What I have said already is true. Khalida is the oldest living that I brought over. The fact that her hair changed from the black hair of her native people to flame red at the time she came over gives credence to the prophecy. The other part of that old prophecy that is never mentioned is I am the one who fed from her and made her a vampire. I am the one who made her hair turn."

Richard leaned back in his chair, his hand rubbing his chin. "So if the prophecy is that she is going to rule our world, and you created her..."

"You know what the norms call one that makes kings?" asked Demetri, pausing to give Richard time to think. "Emperor."

"I can see why you want to keep that to yourself," said Richard. "Some might think your plans too grandiose."

"I know I can trust you to keep this between us. We're getting to the point where I need someone who knows the bigger picture, and can put my requests and plans into perspective," said Demetri.

"It definitely puts a larger emphasis on finding Khalida," said Richard.

"Exactly," said Demetri. He got up from behind his desk and walked around to sit on the edge of the front. "And once we have her, and firmly on our side, we can make sure the prophecy is more widely known. These children are too busy playing midnight supermen, reveling in their strength and power to bother learning the history and lore."

"It could draw an army of vampires to you," said Richard, his voice tinted with a touch of awe.

Demetri smiled. He could see that Richard's eyes had been opened to the bigger picture.

"Perception is reality," said Demetri.

"It's fantastic," said Richard. "The way the pieces can be integrated to not only bring to pass the fulfillment of the prophecy, but elevate you above the prophecy."

"So, shall we go see if Adam has found anything?" Demetri asked as he stood.

"Yes," Richard said, speaking with more enthusiasm and heading for the door faster than normal.

Adam's office was on the floor below Demetri's, and quite a bit smaller. There was a clean desk facing the door, but he was turned at a second computer desk with his back to the door, staring into the computer monitor, his hands flashing across the keyboard. Demetri and Richard stepped in without Adam noticing.

"Any luck?" Demetri asked.

Adam jerked away from the computer. He turned to look at Demetri, obviously startled.

Demetri couldn't help but chuckle. "Better watch your back. Next time you might not be in a protected area."

"Sorry," said Adam. "I was just really into these search procedures I'm running. I've been fine tuning them."

Demetri and Richard sat in the two guest chairs in front of Adam's desk.

"What have you found?" asked Demetri.

"Well, I started with a broad search, but that got me too many hits," said Adam. He pointed to the computer screen as he spoke as if he were referring to a colleague.

"So I worked up a script that would perform the

search and look into each hit for certain key words. Things like 'mysterious circumstances,' 'dead body,' and even 'vampire.' I also have it reject certain words. I was able to rule out drug and gang related murders."

"Anything popping out at you?"

"Lots," said Adam. "So I took the results and grouped them by regional location and date. I've still got *a lot* of results, but I'm starting to eyeball them."

"That's pretty impressive," said Demetri. He knew how to toss a bone to a whipped puppy when he did a good job.

"Thanks. And to answer your question, there are a couple of things that stand out. I was going to work for a couple more hours and then bring my results in progress to you," said Adam.

"I appreciate your dedication to this. Since we're here, what have you got so far?"

Adam turned back to his computer screen. He entered a few keystrokes and brought up a list. He pointed to seven entries grouped together and highlighted in yellow.

"These are articles about missing hikers in the western part of Colorado. They're all within a hundred miles of each other in remote country, and they have occurred over the last three years."

Demetri pondered the screen. "Can you show the area on a map?"

Adam brought up another browser window. With a few keystrokes and mouse clicks he was able to bring up a map of western Colorado on his screen. He used the back end of a pen to point out an area on the screen.

"Here is the area. Like I said, not a lot there."

Demetri looked closer, thinking back to what he knew of Khalida's past. "Weren't there some mining towns back in there?"

"I don't know," said Adam. "I'd have to research it a bit, mapping any towns or camps that used to exist against where the missing hikers cars were found. I'm just curious, but why?"

"I remember Khalida telling me about working as a dance hall dancer in that area a little over a hundred years ago. She said they were hard-rock mining for gold and silver. It's possible that she's in that area now. The caves would provide her shelter during the day as well as a place to stash the bodies of hikers that provided her with fresh human blood."

"Wow, that's a real possibility. It would also explain why no one has been able to find her," Adam observed. "I'll add this lead to the hot file to be followed up on."

"Good. Anything else?" asked Demetri.

"No, not really," said Adam. "That was my hottest lead so far, but it's still early in my search. The only other item that came to my attention isn't related to Khalida, but I was going to pass it on to Richard for someone to verify."

"What is it?" asked Richard, leaning forward so he could see the monitor better.

"It's an article that came up in the big search, but was so recent I started reading it," Adam said as his hand moved the mouse and brought up the web site for an independent newspaper in Los Angeles.

"In summary, it's about some norms finding a dead body outside a club a couple of days ago. It was odd in that someone took off with the body before the police got there. However, the norms took some pictures with a camera phone. Look..." Adam had finished bringing up the article and leaned back out of the way so Demetri and Richard could see the photographs.

Richard excused himself for a minute and left the room. While he was gone Demetri moved to the other side of the desk and read the article. He was almost done when Richard returned, a file folder in his hand.

Richard placed the open folder on the desk. A printed page with Lucrecia's photo and contact information was attached to the left side. "The photos in the article aren't the best, but between them and the descriptions I think it might be Lucrecia, one of the operatives we sent to L.A."

Demetri looked at the photo in the file and the one on the computer screen. "I think you're right. It says someone took her before the police got there. It's possible she's not really dead. When did she check in last?"

Richard flipped up the contact sheet and looked at the next page. "She's overdue to report in by twenty-four hours. Her last entry says she was going to reconnoiter the Goth club scene; however, for a lot of our operatives that usually means ten percent work and ninety percent party."

"The article says she was found near a Goth club," said Adam, "but it doesn't say anything about her being at the club."

"But the ones who found her had been there, so it couldn't have been too far away. Does it mention the name of the club?" said Demetri.

Adam turned back to the article and scanned it. "No, it always refers to it as the club, but it gives a cross street. Hang on."

Demetri watched as Adam brought up another window and entered the streets mentioned in the article. Soon a map came up that showed a two-mile section in LA. Adam made a few more clicks and turned back.

"Okay, I've got three zip codes used in that area. Just another check," Adam said.

Back at his keyboard Adam brought up the phone company directory assistance page. He put in to search for nightclubs in the three zip codes. Several entries came back, but he turned back quickly.

"I see what happened. There is a club that's named The Club, and it's location is the one described in the article," said Adam.

Demetri was impressed. "Good work. Richard, is there anything in her reports that give any significance to The Club?"

Richard flipped through the pages in Lucrecia's file. "No, nothing at all."

Demetri needed more information. "Adam, have there been any follow up articles with this or other papers? Or other media for that matter."

Adam turned back to work on his computer. The clack of the keyboard filled the background while Demetri spoke with Richard.

"Something happened to her when she went to that club," Demetri said.

"But the lack of a body, or even ashes, doesn't help us," said Richard.

"No other articles," said Adam over his shoulder.

"Is there any way to find out more information about The Club?"

Demetri watched as Adam ran through web sites faster than he could follow. Results would pop up and Adam was branching off or rerunning searches as soon as the screen was displayed.

Adam turned back to them. "Okay, they don't have a web site, or at least not one easily associated with their name. Their name is so generic that the searches I enter for the name and area still give me thousands of hits."

Demetri shook his head. He hated being stymied. "What about the paper that had the article. It sounds like the kind that would cover the clubs and nightlife. What if you just searched there?"

"That was the search that got me the fewest hits, but it was still over five hundred," said Adam.

Demetri leaned back over Adam's shoulder, reading the article again. The article was on the right hand side of the screen with menu options for the site on the left. Demetri pointed to one of the links. "What does 'Ad Images' mean?"

Adam clicked on the link. Images of advertisements that had appeared in the print edition were shown. Scrolling down the page they were able to look at all of the ads.

Demetri followed the scroll of ads. He saw the ad at what must have been the same time Adam did, because the younger vampire stopped scrolling. The ad was for The Club, and had a picture of their feature band, Sinister Sisters.

"Khalida Raven is what happened to her," said Demetri as he stabbed his finger on the screen. "I want a printout of that ad and everything you can find on Sinister Sisters."

Demetri turned back to Richard, the excitement of the hunt coming back to him. His quarry in his sights. "Lucrecia went there to party, and was spotted by Khalida. Remember it was after the show that the body was found. She lured Lucrecia to the alley and killed her. She must have friends there, someone to haul the body away to keep attention away from the club. It makes sense."

"It also means she isn't operating alone out there," said Richard. "Someone is helping her."

Adam handed Demetri a printout of the ad. Looking down at it Demetri pondered the variables. "I think I know who. There's only one vampire out there that has the resources for a fast snatch at the last minute like this."

"Dafyd Peack," said Richard.

"Exactly," said Demetri. "I know we've just started preliminary scouting trips, but perhaps I should pay them a visit."

"Do you think that's wise? Let's send someone else. It's too early for you to take a personal interest in his group," Richard said.

"That may be, but there is too much at stake," Demetri said as he worked out sound, non-threatening business reasons why he would need to go to the West Coast.

"Okay, it's obvious that Khalida has taken steps to keep what happened to Lucrecia away from her hangout. She must feel safe since the police have obviously not bothered to investigate. They must think this is a prank by those Goths."

Demetri paced in the confines of Adam's office. He watched his feet as he shuffled back and forth. He was not naïve enough to think that Peack didn't know who he was or what he was doing, even if he'd never done more than send preliminary scouts to LA.

"Okay, let's set it up this way. I go out on the next night flight to LA, with only four others. I make direct contact with Peack and tell him I am looking for one of my people that had been from that area and was taking a vacation. I tell him I came myself so he wouldn't think it was an invasion from my organization. What do you think?"

"Plausible," said Richard. "But what if he doesn't buy it?"

"Ah, that's part two," said Demetri. "While I'm there with minimal support and trying to convince them of what I want them to perceive me as, we fly in a couple dozen agents from our locations around the country the next night."

Demetri stopped pacing. "And while they think I'm looking for Lucrecia, we can make a snatch and grab of our own," he said as he jabbed the picture of Khalida in his hand.

CHAPTER TEN

Raven and Cowboy stood on the street in front of the office building, the sky was dark but the sidewalk well lit from streetlights. Despite the fact that it was seven o'clock, over half of the windows had lights shining bright. Raven stepped into the lobby and looked over the directory. The building was four stories tall and according to the directory housed the offices of several types of doctors, three attorneys, and a combination private detective bounty hunter among other tenants.

"I have to say, this wasn't the type of place I expected to find a Shaman," said Cowboy.

"Let me guess, you were expecting a run-down storefront, the front glass dirty and cluttered with dusty fake ancient relics from Egypt," said Raven.

"Actually I was hoping for naked dancing on the top of a mountain," joked Cowboy.

Raven punched him in the arm. "In your dreams, Slick."

Cowboy looked over the directory. "I don't see any

Shaman listed. Which one is it?"

"Right here," said Raven. She pointed to the listing for Herbal Medicine Inc. on the fourth floor.

"Huh. Sounds like one of those network marketing companies," said Cowboy.

"No, I'm pretty sure it's a Shaman," said Raven.

Cowboy looked at her. "Pretty sure?"

"Well, I haven't actually been here before," said Raven.

"If you've never been here before, how do you know that's a Shaman?" asked Cowboy, his tone one of disbelief.

"Two reasons," said Raven. She plucked at Cowboy's sleeve and led him back outside. She pointed up at a window on the top floor. "One, look up at the fourth floor. That window second from the corner. See that symbol in the window? My people had no real written language, but we did have symbols for key things. That is symbol that was used to mark the tent of the Shaman."

"Raven darlin', that could have been copied from anywhere. A lot of those new-agers do that sort of thing."

"True, but remember what I said. We didn't have a written language. We didn't have printing like the invading white man," said Raven. "But I thought of that, too, and so the second reason I know there is a Shaman there is I had her checked out."

"Her?"

"Yes. I saw that symbol one night and investigated. I may be a vampire but I've kept tabs on what has happened to my people over the years. She is the granddaughter of the Shaman of a tribe that absorbed my people centuries ago."

"Absorbed?" asked Cowboy.

"Okay, conquered. I was hoping you'd let me have my pride even euphemistically. Let's go in," said Raven.

When they stepped into the office it could have been that of any business. There was a receptionist desk complete with computer and multi-line phone. A couch and chairs arranged around a low table provided seating for six people and magazines to occupy them while they waited. The lights were on, but there was no one at the receptionist desk.

"I'll be right with you," a voiced called from an open door behind the receptionist desk.

Raven stood in the center of the room, watching the open door. Cowboy sat on the edge of the couch and flipped through the magazines, pausing to read the covers before moving on to the next.

"Now, how can I help you," said a woman as she stepped through the open door. She appeared to be in her mid-fifties. Her hair had gone gray, but was styled in a cut that kept it off her shoulders. She wore black slacks and a light blue sweater. A gold necklace lay over the sweater.

Raven looked at the woman, and when they made eye contact the woman stopped speaking and moving forward. Raven watched to see what the woman would do. This was the final test.

"I don't have what you need here," said the woman.

"And what would that be?" asked Raven.

The woman didn't move except to look between Raven

and Cowboy. Raven could see her swallow, clearing her mouth and throat before speaking.

"I have nothing here. This isn't a doctor's office. We don't take or give blood," she said.

Raven stared deeply into the woman's eyes. "You know who we are. Tell me."

The woman looked from Raven to Cowboy, and then to the phone on the receptionist desk. "I have never done anything to you or any of yours."

"Tell me," said Raven, taking a step toward the woman.

The woman stepped back. "Vampires," she said in a hushed tone.

Raven turned to Cowboy. "That completes my third check," she said.

"How so?" asked Cowboy.

"She knew who we were before we said or did anything. Not regular customers, and not humans of questionable motives based on our clothing," said Raven, ignoring the looks of confusion she was getting from the woman.

"Please don't hurt me," said the woman.

Raven turned back to the woman. "Oh course not. I have come to speak to you in your tribal capacity."

"I don't understand," said the woman.

Raven pointed to the window that contained the diagram of the Shaman.

"You know the symbol? I am a shaman for my tribe, but you are not known to me. I don't know how I can help you," the woman said.

"Were you taught the oral histories?" Raven asked. The woman only nodded.

Raven stood tall. "I am Bright Sea Bird, daughter of Chief Striking Bearclaw, granddaughter of Chief Swifthorse."

Raven watched as the woman thought over what Raven had said. She could see her lips moving as she ran through the litany of the history. Raven knew she had reached her father when her eyes grew wide.

"That would make you almost four hundred years old," she said.

"Give or take a few," said Raven.

"But why have you come to me? I have no medicines for your kind," said the woman.

"Please, let us go into your office and sit. You have nothing to fear from the two of us," said Raven.

Once seated Raven spoke again. "First, no one in this city really knows my history. I have come here seeking refuge from another of my kind who wishes to control me. I ask that you keep this information secret."

"As if anyone would believe me if I were to tell," said the woman.

"There are those who would believe you," said Cowboy.

"My name is Amy Dakota Gunston. I trained as a Shaman at the knee of my grandfather Two Feathers Gunston. I will tell no one you have been here."

"Thank you," said Raven. "I have not come for any medicines. As you say your powders would not be of any use to me. But my father taught me that the Shaman of the tribe should be consulted for advice. Particularly if there is a coming battle."

"There is a battle coming?" asked Amy.

"I don't know," said Raven. "I've established myself in this city, and live among the norms, excuse me, humans as if one of them."

"But that has changed," said Amy.

"I don't know. A vampire that I have not seen before, bearing the mark of the one that wishes to control me, was killed in the city recently. Her body was seen near where I work."

"And you fear she was here looking for you."

"This other has always been seeking me since I escaped him. My fear is that she found me, knew me, and reported my presence to him," said Raven.

"This is kind of out of my area as a Shaman," said Amy. "There haven't been a lot of war councils of late. Most of my advisory work has been on relationships. But let me think about this."

Raven watched as Amy closed her eyes. Soon Amy was rocking in place, a barely audible chant coming from her. Raven picked up the chant and joined in. She swayed her body and closed her eyes. Images of sitting under the night sky came to her mind. A huge bonfire filled the center of a clearing. Smoke and sparks rose to the winds and were carried away. Raven heard the sounds of many voices taking up the chant. Looking around inside her vision Raven saw many others join around the bonfire. She did not recognize anyone and was about to move to see the others on the other side of the fire better when the chanting stopped.

Raven opened her eyes and saw Amy staring at her, but her eyes were not focusing. Sweat ran down the side of Amy's face. She sat with her hands flat on the desk in front of her, her muscles rigid and tense.

"Are you okay?" Raven asked.

Amy sucked in a deep breath and let it out. Raven realized that Amy had not been breathing. She saw when Amy's eyes came back into focus.

"It has never been that strong before," said Amy in a hushed, reverent tone.

"I want to feel sad," said Raven, "it was so beautiful. But I don't feel sad. I felt safe, uplifted."

"Yes," said Amy. "That was the vision for you. It was so clear and strong. There is a strength that is part of your being."

"But what did it mean?" asked Raven.

Amy licked her lips before speaking. "In my vision I was a crow sitting in a tree at the edge of a clearing. I saw you sitting by a bonfire chanting. As you chanted others came into the clearing to join you. Their voices joined yours and the chant became a shout of protection."

"I was there, in the field next to the fire," said Raven.

"As to the meaning, the normal interpretation would be that there is strength and safety with the tribe," said Amy.

"My tribe?" said Raven. "My tribe has long been assimilated into other tribes. I would not know where to find any of them. I found you only by your mark."

"I said it was the normal interpretation. You are different. Your tribe is different now. The vision is applied to your new kind, but the core message is still the same. There is safety in numbers."

"Safety in numbers... new tribe..." Raven said, thinking out loud. "But I'm trying to not get taken into the clutches of this vampire. I want to stay out of his tribe."

"Tell me, does this vampire have enemies?" Amy asked.

Cowboy broke his silence. "He has killed many of his enemies, but still has many more."

"There is an old saying. It may not be from our culture, but I think it applies now," said Amy. "The enemy of my enemy is my friend."

"The enemy of my enemy is my friend," repeated Raven.

"Is there one who could become your friend? Someone with power and can provide the strength of numbers?"

"I don't know," said Raven. "I've worked hard to stay away from the other vampires in this city."

Cowboy cleared his throat. "I may know one."

CHAPTER ELEVEN

"Demetri is on his way," Gabrielle said. "He's taking the red-eye out and should land at approximately 4:45 this morning."

Every vampire that was part of Peack's Projects had gathered in what had at one time been a ballroom and was now the main parlor of the big house. Like the blue parlor it had a luxurious ambiance that disguised its use as a tactical conference room. The overstuffed antique chairs had been arranged for this occasion into a series of loose semi-circles, with low tables positioned so as to permit good viewing for all. They faced the large panel screen on the wall, and away from the blackout curtains. A few well-placed plants, a scattering of desks and entertainment centers along the walls, the heavily padded carpet, and expensive art hanging on the walls completed the parlor setting.

Dafyd Peack sat at the computer operating the large panel screen. The facts as they knew them, as they had been able to gather them, were displayed for all to see.

A column of bullets demarking what little they knew, and ending with no solution.

He knew that appearance didn't mean as much as abilities, Dafyd still worried about how he presented himself to his people. Not having a solution bothered him more than the gray in his hair or his stocky build that some might call stout. However, he had no more control over how he appeared than over obtaining a solution to this problem. That was why he played the game as he did. To play to people's strengths and to their abilities, rather than their weaknesses and shortcomings.

"So," Dafyd said into the silence. "That is what we know. Let's start generating ideas. We only have a few hours."

Dafyd and the team leaders, Flavian, Monique, Nguyen, Oscar, Petra, and Gabrielle, remained silent waiting for their people to take the opportunity to speak, before they pronounced their own ideas. Which ideas would have to be implemented.

"Is there anywhere we haven't looked for the yokel that Lucrecia left the club with?" someone asked.

"There are a lot of places left." Nguyen stood; a slender man, originally Vietnamese, he was too soft spoken to be easily heard if he remained seated. "Every vampire hunter organization, a good deal of the college campuses, most of LA's club scene. It is easier to list where we have looked. He hasn't been to any hospital, police station, or medical clinic. He hasn't been back to that club, any other club within a five-mile radius, or any other Goth club in the city. Unfortunately, we have no name, no photograph, and only a vague description. We don't know if he is associated with the men who took her away in the van, or if he disappeared before they arrived on the scene."

"I would suggest that we assume he is associated with the men that took her away," one of the L.A. team said. "This assumption helps to limit our search area."

"Exactly why we shouldn't." Kayze bounced around in her chair, twisting to face the other speaker, flinging her long brown hair as her head turned. She resembled nothing so much as a hyperactive teenager. "I realize we don't have much time, but since we haven't found him yet, we need to widen our search area."

"Is there any way we can do a search correlating the partial license plate with average looking yokels?"

"Unfortunately," Oscar said, "the government doesn't collect such descriptions to go with the ownership of motor vehicles." He had remained seated. His booming voice matched his extensive frame, and needed no amplification to be heard throughout the room.

Kayze stood, swinging her long hair, her brown eyes searching for the questioner. "And two of our witnesses saw him leave with Lucrecia, and they didn't see him with the men who took her in the van. So even assuming he is associated with the kidnappers, he probably doesn't own the van."

"The most likely scenario," a young, male, leather-clad, vampire said, "is that the men who kidnapped her were vampire hunters. Do we have any plans to attack and search *their* lairs?"

"They could just as easily have been a gang looking for an easy mark to attack and rape," an older, female, vampire said. "Or a gang that hates Goths. Or a bunch out for a criminal joyride. Or just plain idiots that accidentally killed her and were trying to cover their tracks."

Nguyen stood and held up a hand to stop the arguments starting to flow around the room. "There are many possibilities. The vampire hunters *are* the most likely." No one else tried to speak over him, simply because they respected him. "However, attacking each and every group in the city is bound to both get us much unwanted attention and at least one of us would be hurt or killed. And we still might not find Lucrecia. In fact, if the kidnappers *were* vampire hunters, the chances of us finding her at this point are almost non-existent. She'd probably be nothing more than ash in the backyard."

A voice spoke up. "We need to secure our defense against Demetri, rather than waste time foolishly debating the fate of one vampire."

Dafyd looked around to see who had spoken. He didn't recognize the woman. She appeared to be middle-aged, with an oddly unremarkable appearance, as if she normally tried to fade into the background. He caught Oscar nodding his head, and assumed she was one of his people; Dafyd already began to consider stealing her away for headquarters. He preferred to work with people who knew how to cut through the extraneous to the heart of a problem.

But the arguments rose again.

"If the security of the organization is more important than the survival of one individual, then we should storm the vampire hunters' lairs."

"That's not security."

"We'll have to implement our crises security protocols."

"If Demetri's spies are as good as everyone says they are then separating our leaders will allow him to pick them off one by one."

"He'll have to find them first, and that'll be harder if they're not all huddled together making it easy for him."

"Perhaps we can reason with this Demetri. Perhaps if we give him a show of good faith, he'll back down."

"I wouldn't give him the time of day. I used to live in New York, back when he first started consolidating. The only 'reason' he'll understands is accompanied by unconditional surrender."

Dafyd looked to his team leaders. Without speaking they all seemed to agree that the rabble needed a little longer to hash it out, before being brought to heel. In any case, something useful might actually pop out.

"Perhaps a show of power. If we grab all of Vasile's remaining spies, that will cut off his knowledge base, and put us in a better bargaining position."

"And why should we hand him a reason to attack us? So far we've done nothing to him, or his operation."

"He doesn't need a reason. For all we know he had his own people kidnap her so that he'd have an excuse."

That idea got all the team leaders thinking. They all reached for their cells, and began a secret conclave through text messaging on their cells. Dafyd had suspected they would do that during this meeting.

"It'd be something he'd do." Petra sent the first message.

"Down to making certain someone witnessed it, and that we couldn't find either kidnappers or kidnappee," Flavian replied from his cell.

"It would give him an excellent excuse to invade. Something no one would question," Nguyen sent next.

"Admirably devious. We must include this scenario in our response," Oscar sent.

While the leaders hashed this out silently on their cells, the rest of the assembled vampires had continued their increasingly loud and wide-ranging argument.

Someone decided to speak loudly in order to be heard over the murmuring. "He won't bring that many people with him into our territory, not at first. We have to crush him the minute he sets foot in LA. Before he is able to bring in a large enough force to crush us."

"The best defense is a good offense."

"Only in certain types of games."

"That does apply in war."

"Do we want to allow him to set the terms of the game along with setting the locale?"

"The game is the game. He's not setting that."

"He is if we just let him play war, rather than forcing him to play something else."

"You're an idiot!"

"Enough!" Dafyd shouted. And the room went silent, all eyes trained on their leader. "We do not ridicule anyone or anyone's ideas. This is a brainstorming session. We need everyone to contribute, and name calling won't further that agenda."

"I have an idea," an older vampire said. "Most of the world's people believe in those who are wiser and better in tune with life and the world—prophets, seers, sorcerers, witches, saints, divines. There are many names for them. Perhaps it is time for us to see if there are any among us vampires."

The assembled looked amongst themselves, some chuckling, some rolling their eyes, some seriously considering it.

"Maybe he's volunteering?" Kayze asked, looking at the old man.

The old man laughed. "Not me. It's not age or years that make you wise. It is something intrinsic to the being."

"Perhaps we should check every old prophecy we can find. Maybe there's something in one of them that would help."

A younger male vampire jumped up onto his chair. "Everyone drop your pants so we can check for oddly shaped birthmarks on everyone's buttocks," he laughed. "While we're at it, we probably should give everyone a thorough examination."

"You wish," Kayze muttered.

"There are plenty of prophecies concerning, vampires."

"I'd rather rely on our strength, our numbers, our loyalties, and our abilities, rather than the incomprehensible ramblings of ancient witchdoctors that were high on who-knows-what."

"However," Dafyd said bringing the debate to a close, "there is no harm in pursuing all options open to us. Monique see if you can find someone in our records who might fit the bill as a wise man or woman."

Short and perky, with blonde hair and pale eyes that

made her more washed out than beautiful, Monique worked hard to convey strength and intelligence by wearing business power suits, in black of course. "I know of several, in and out of our organization." Monique made a few notes onto her hand-held. "I'll get back to you."

"Nguyen?" Dafyd waved his hand to indicate that he had the floor.

Standing, Nguyen said, "The L.A. team will continue to search for Lucrecia and her mysterious kidnappers. We will have some sort of information about Lucrecia before Demetri arrives, and hopefully will be able to pinpoint her kidnappers for him."

Dafyd nodded. "Oscar?"

Oscar didn't bother to rise from his chair, but he did shift his bulk in it. "My analysts and I will head to a secure location, to continue sorting data as we receive it. We will give consideration to all ideas put forth in this brainstorming session. No matter who put the idea forth, and no matter how outlandish the idea seems." He nodded to the old man. "And we will be researching old prophecies."

"Very good." Dafyd turned to Gabrielle. "And on the business-side?"

The epitome of the stereotypical old, white-haired lawyer that she was, Gabrielle's thin, pinched face puckered as her lips pursed in thought. An affectation Dafyd expected of her; he knew she'd already thought through anything she was going to say and had weighed each word. When she finally opened her mouth, Gabrielle said, "We will continue our stock diversification and business acquisition, in anticipation of Peack's Projects' continuation. We have a very promising prospect for franchising, if we can convince the current owner of the lucrative possibilities." Gabrielle smiled. "Very lucrative possibilities."

Ah yes, Dafyd remembered when he'd been the business team leader. That had always been fun. "Flavian?" He turned and acknowledged the oldest among them who seemed to think it necessary to maintain the archetype appearance and manners expected of vampires. Flavian's sophisticated bearing and ultra-polite manners were well matched to his long, elegant, and classical appearance, as well as his cultured voice. "Intelligence operations will continue to funnel data to the analysis team. We'll co-ordinate with security and the LA team to find Lucrecia, and keep everyone aware of Vasile's movements. And I'll add the acquisition of prophecies and location of seers to the desired data lists for all operatives." Flavian opened one elegant hand as if passing the proverbial ball back to Dafyd.

"Headquarters will remain open. We will establish a line of communication with Demetri Vasile. We will be the front for all contact with Vasile." Dafyd grinned. "And as far as Vasile is concerned we will pretend to know nothing of Lucrecia or her kidnapping, under the assumption that it was all instigated by Vasile as a ruse to attack us. We will play the ignorant innocents. Security?"

Petra stood. A large, commanding woman, Petra looked like a body builder or perhaps a tank. There were rumors that she'd been in the military before becoming a vampire. She always wore camouflage pants and a loose jacket with lots of pockets, clothes that hid her weapons and armor. She kept her hair short and her group neat as a pin. "As of this moment the entire organization is on the crisis security level. Team leaders will be accompanied by four bodyguards at all times. All team leaders will choose and announce a successor and inform the others. After a final team-leader meeting, of no more than fifteen minutes, all team leaders will disperse to their designated secure locations, and until such time as the security level has been lowered, team leaders will not meet face to face anywhere at any time. All teams will be in voice and data contact with all other teams at their secure locations. Any loss of contact will be reported to security immediately. All teams are to get their specific orders from their team leader." She looked around the silent room for a moment. "Disperse!"

It seemed that everyone started talking at once, but at least they were leaving. In less than two minutes, Petra informed Dafyd after she timed it. Only the seven team leads remained and they gathered around the computer desk, except for Oscar, who remained in his seat not far away.

Dafyd shook his head. "Are we really reduced to prophecies and seers?"

Flavian laughed. "Reduced to, no. But every little bit helps. You just never know."

"Be careful how you handle Vasile," Oscar warned.

"Yes," Dafyd said. "I'll have to break out the tongs and the ten foot pole."

"He may get one or more of us," Petra said, "but the

organization will survive to fight him. It'll take more than the loss of one piece to win the game."

"Let us all sincerely hope so," Monique said.

"I always wondered what would happen if ancient Greek philosophy clashed with ancient Chinese wisdom," Nguyen said.

"One would hope the ancients were smarter than that," Gabrielle said.

Oscar finally rose from his chair. "This game has been going for a long, long time. Even the ancients played it."

Nguyen shrugged. "Actually, what I've really wondered is which of all the philosophies conveys the most advantage."

"A riddle for another time," Petra said. "Perhaps Oscar's analysts could figure it out."

"Only given appropriate data." Oscar sighed and started lumbering toward the door. The others followed him.

"Good luck all," Flavian said.

"The game's afoot," Nguyen said.

Monique groaned. "Not that old thing."

"It's not that old," Nguyen said.

Dafyd watched them leave, wondering which among them wouldn't return. Even if the loss of one piece didn't mean the loss of the game, it would still be a loss. Dafyd had come to respect and treasure each and every one of them.

CHAPTER TWELVE

Raven began to get nervous as she and Cowboy approached a large mansion. It was well lit, and seemed to be crowded. As Cowboy parked in a spot after another car pulled out, she could see there were lots of people leaving the mansion. Some were obviously vampires, and the others could have been, but it was hard to tell at a distance.

"Are you sure this is the best place to go for help?"

"Trust me," said Cowboy. "Dafyd is the most connected vampire in this part of the state."

Raven must have let her fear show on her face. Cowboy looked at her and said, "Don't worry, he's nothing like Demetri."

Raven tried to smile, but she couldn't help but feel nervous. After so many years of hiding in one form or another, working hard to stay under the radar and out of the notice of other vampires, it was hard to give that up. She only hoped that Cowboy really knew this Dafyd as well as he thought he did.

The mansion was beautiful, the kind of beautiful the rich and famous had gravitated to for longer than Raven had been alive. The style was Victorian, but too new to have actually been built during that time period; it must have been built by someone who made some bucks in town, and built a house to remind them of the home they had left behind for LA.

Raven was relieved to see that all of the vampires they had recently seen were leaving the area. She tried to look casual as she took Cowboy's arm when they got out of his car. She took a deep breath to calm herself. The scent of the flowers and other plants landscaping the property filled and comforted her. She had been born into a people that were a part of the forest. It had stayed with her.

She tried to relax, but had to keep from bolting when Cowboy rang the doorbell.

Cowboy squeezed her arm, feeling her nervousness and said. "Let me introduce you and we'll see what happens from there."

"I know you're trying to help, but I can't help but feel like I'm about to walk into the sunrise," she said.

The door opened to reveal a female vampire standing in a large entryway. She looked to be in her mid-thirties in human terms. She wore a loose white top, a sort of sun dress done as a shirt over pressed blue jeans and sandals. She looked at Raven first, quizzical, then turned to Cowboy and smiled.

"Hi. Lincoln isn't it?" she asked.

"Yes, ma'am. Sorry to intrude, but I was wondering if Dafyd could spare a few minutes."

"Come in, and let me see what he's up to," she said

as she opened the door wider letting them both enter.

She closed the door behind them. "If you wouldn't mind waiting here, I'll see if he's available."

Raven tried not to think of herself as a trapped animal as the woman left. She tried to focus on the area around her. The entryway was a large room about twenty square feet. Hallways went off to the left and right, and a staircase to the second floor was centered on the wall in front of them. There was a stone fountain gurgling water to the left of the staircase, and a full suit of armor in a matching position on the right side. Raven was studying the two items and the mosaic stone tile floor that was under them.

"I call them war and peace," said a voice behind her.

Raven turned and met the eyes of a vampire that looked physically just a little older than the one that had answered the door. But to Raven the eyes belied the age of the body. Here was someone old, mature, someone that had been around a long time.

"Excuse me?" Raven said.

"The fountain and the armor. I call them war and peace," the vampire said.

"They're nice," Raven said because she felt something was expected but she didn't know what else to day.

"Thank you," said the vampire before turning to Cowboy. "Lincoln, always a pleasure to see you. Everything going well, I hope?"

"Everything's fine. We're on track to have the three standard-sized rooms completed on schedule. I'm still working out the designs for the party room you requested. I'll bring the plans by in a couple of days," said Cowboy as they shook hands.

"Good, good. I have to confess I wasn't expecting you tonight. Did I forget to write down an appointment?"

"I'm sorry, where are my manners," said Cowboy. "I brought my friend here to meet you. Raven, this is Dafyd Peack. Dafyd, this is Raven, a good friend for over a hundred years."

Raven extended her hand, and felt Dafyd's strong grip.

"Any friend of Lincoln's is welcome here," said Dafyd.

"Thank you," Raven said. She was still nervous about being in this man's house. He seemed nice enough, and Cowboy hadn't steered her wrong before.

"Dafyd is the one who is buying my thrill rooms out here," said Cowboy. "He even came up with an idea to build a much larger room so it can be used for hosting parties."

"I've mentioned it to a few people and they can't wait," Dafyd said.

"I might be a bit biased, but it'll knock their socks off. One thing I was going to talk to you about later is that the large rooms will probably work best if we don't have them move. There'll be too many people in the room to key off all of them, and tying it to one person could give the others a bit of vertigo if they are standing still and the world is moving around them."

Raven watched Dafyd, trying to read him. He seemed genuinely interested in Cowboy's vampire thrill rooms. His eyes squinted a bit, and he pursed his lips while Cowboy was talking.

"Hmm, that may not be that bad," Dafyd said. "We

could still set up outdoor party sequences, static scenes in meadows, mountain tops, city parks, almost anywhere in the world. Oh, and being static should cut down on production costs and time for the video experience."

"That it would," Cowboy confirmed.

"Weather," Raven interjected.

Dafyd turned toward her. "Excuse me."

Raven hadn't realized she had spoken it aloud. Ever since Cowboy had told her about his invention she had thought about it in the back of her mind. To experience the outdoors realistically in even fake sunlight sounded divine.

"I'm sorry, I didn't mean to stick my nose in," said Raven.

"No, Raven, go ahead," said Cowboy. "What were you thinking?"

"It's just a personal thing, but one of the joys of outdoors for me is weather, how it changes. Life is enhanced by the changing weather. I for one have had too much rain only at night."

"I've designed the programs to include wind gusts and breezes, even carrying birdsong so it sounds like birds are flying," Cowboy said.

"It sounds great, but what if you hooked in sprinklers?" asked Raven. She closed her eyes to picture herself in a field. "The sky darkens, and lightning flashes across the horizon. Thunder rumbles, felt in the body not just the ears. A fresh spring rain falls, drenching the trees and grass around you, your clothes so wet they weigh you down, sticking against your skin. And the sun comes out again, warming your skin, drying your clothes. Birds sing and the air is clean, free from the scent of fire, smoke, and animals."

Raven took a deep breath and opened her eyes. She had allowed her nerves to let her jabber on, and now she felt like a fool. Cowboy and Dafyd were staring at her; she could read disbelief on their faces.

"I'm sorry, I shouldn't have gone on like that," Raven said.

"I could sell tickets to that performance," Dafyd said. "Lincoln, I want it. Just like she described. Can you do it?"

Cowboy nodded. "I think I could rig it pretty easily. Even have distinctive rains from light showers to gully washers."

Cowboy turned to Raven. "Any more ideas, darlin'?"

"Snow," said Raven. "Can you get one of those machines that make snow? I think a morning with fresh snow on the ground, the air so cool you can see your breath. The crystallized top of the snow sparkling like jewels cast across the snow."

Dafyd shook his head. "Lincoln, she's thinking outside of boxes you haven't seen yet. You better get her signed onto your team before she becomes a competitor."

Raven politely laughed, feeling even more embarrassed. She hated when she got nervous. She never knew what to say and always ended up saying too much. At least she didn't have to worry about Cowboy thinking she was trying to steal his ideas. He was laughing along with her and Dafyd.

As the laugh settled down Dafyd said, "Lincoln,

thanks for he update. Now I'm looking forward to these rooms even more. When you come back, remind me to tell you about some franchise ideas I've got."

Dafyd took a step toward the door and stretched his hand out, indicating the way to the door. Raven was automatically taking a step toward the door when Cowboy spoke up.

"Actually Dafyd, I came by tonight so Raven could talk to you. Could you spare her a minute?"

Dafyd glanced as his watch. "Sure. I've got some time. Let's go up and find a place to sit."

Raven followed Dafyd with Cowboy bringing up the rear, going up the stairs to the second floor. Dafyd led them to a small sitting room with four overstuffed leather chairs. They took seats.

"What can I do for you, Raven?" Dafyd asked.

"First, I just want to say I'm sorry to intrude on you—"

Dafyd made shushing hand motions toward her. "Don't worry about it. Just tell me what you need to tell me."

"Okay, well, I know that you are an important vampire here, and I'm almost afraid to tell you that I've been living in the area for a while now. But I've been keeping a low profile," she confessed.

"There's nothing wrong with that. Our kind tends to be loners, living on the fringe. I'm more of an anomaly, gathering other vampires together," said Dafyd. "Would it surprise you to know that I knew who you were when you came in tonight?"

Raven felt a cold knife sticking in her gut. She nodded her head. "Yes, it would. I haven't approached any other vampires, and have worked hard to mask my identity."

"I can tell that bothers you, but don't worry. I'm a businessman, Raven. I have businesses and an organization of vampires that help me run those businesses. The companies I control aren't just for vampire products and services, by the way. I make a healthy profit selling to norms."

Raven allowed herself to relax a little easier.

Dafyd continued, "I don't force people to become members of my organization. Those that join me do so of their own free will. Those that don't, like yourself, are free to live their lives, so long as they don't try to harm me. As such, some of my staff brought you to my attention a while back. They happened to be out clubbing and caught your show. Nothing big. A notation was made in a file. Nothing more."

Raven wasn't sure if that was a good thing or a bad thing, but she tried to picture herself in his shoes and figured it was at least a practical thing. Still, she hoped he wouldn't consider her the problem when she told him her problem.

"I'll be honest that I'm a little nervous," Raven said. "You see, I've been living here, hiding from another vampire that doesn't share your *laissez-faire* attitude. In fact he has a nasty habit of pushing his way into other vampires' business."

"I take it he has found you, or you wouldn't have come to me," said Dafyd.

"That's true. I wouldn't have. But I'm not sure if he's found me," said Raven. "His name is Demetri Vasile, and he runs New York, most of the East Coast, and is branching into the Midwest."

Dafyd nodded. "I've heard of him. You're right, he has a habit of sticking his nose in other people's business. I've heard stories, and when Demetri Vasile is involved, vampire and human alike die."

"And I wouldn't want that to happen to anyone here. I didn't mean to cause any problems, but if he has found me he will come for me," said Raven.

Raven watched Dafyd for a reaction. She wasn't sure if he would just grab her and turn her over to avoid problems with Demetri, or pooh-pooh her worries and send her on her way.

"How long have you been hiding from him?" Dafyd asked.

"About forty years now," said Raven. "I was able to escape from a detention cell he had me locked in."

"Forty years," said Dafyd. "Raven, not to belittle your worries, but what makes you think Demetri is still looking for you? While our kind can live forever, I don't see many grudges going on for decades. Our lives are too full to keep track of pettiness."

Raven looked down at her feet. She found her fingers were working the edge of her shirt, shifting the material back and forth between the fingers. "It's not a grudge," she said. "He thinks I am the fulfillment of prophecy. A prophecy that he is trying to manipulate to rule the world."

"Excuse me?" asked Dafyd, his head slightly cocked as his interest perked up.

Raven stood up and stepped over to the wall feeling better with it at her back. "There was this prophecy ages ago. It said that there would be a vampire that when they were transformed their hair would turn blood red. That vampire was destined to rule the dark empire."

Her hands fluttered in front of her, Raven realized she was waving and shaking her hand and pushed them behind her back.

"The reason he wants me is that Demetri turned me centuries ago. When he fed from me, my hair turned from the black hair all my people had, to the dark red you see now," said Raven. "When he discovered the prophecy he came to me, and that was when he imprisoned me the first time."

"You're kidding," an interested Dafyd said.

"No." She could see Cowboy shaking his head out of the corner of her eyes.

Dafyd was also shaking his head. "I'm sorry. I don't mean to trample on anyone else's beliefs, but does anyone believe this? I mean, some hermit picked the wrong mushrooms one day and suddenly he's a Holy Man with inner sight."

Raven found herself chuckling. "That about sums up my opinion about this too. But Demetri is very single minded in his quest to control me. Frankly, I don't want to be controlled."

"What vampire does?" Dafyd posed. "So why have you come to me? You can always take off, and pick another hiding place."

Raven came back to her chair and sat. "I could," she said, "but I've put down roots here, such as they are. And I'm not certain he knows I'm here. I don't want to take off if I don't have to."

"Practical," said Dafyd.

"Well, the way I see it, based on Demetri's past performance, it would be in both our interests if we knew Demetri was coming to LA."

"I can't argue with that," Dafyd said.

"So I came to tell you about me, and the possibility that I could be drawing him here. I was hoping that we could agree that if either of us gets wind of his actually coming, that we could tell the other," Raven said. She sat holding her breath, afraid she was about to be turned down.

"That sounds reasonable," Dafyd said while he nodded his head. "If you see or hear anything about Demetri you let me know. In turn I'll let you know everything I can."

Raven let out her breath, relief washing over her, the feeling of a knife in her stomach easing.

"Thank you," she said.

CHAPTER THIRTEEN

Demetri shoved past the people who insisted on walking like sluggish blobs stretching across the corridor. He ignored their dirty looks and half spoken words of indignity. Demetri didn't care. Why two people felt they were entitled to take up six feet of a ten-foot wide hallway was beyond him. He wondered if these people had any place to be, or if they routinely came to the airport for leisurely strolls.

It would be dawn soon and Demetri had to get to his hotel or be stuck hiding in the bowels of the airport until nightfall. He was angry and it annoyed him all the more that he couldn't take it out on anybody. There was no one to blame for the delay. At least no one he could get his hands on.

First they were stuck waiting for the door to the airplane to be fixed. The door would close, but the open indicator light would not go off. Demetri sat with the rest of the passengers, while a sleepy-eyed mechanic shuffled around, poking at pieces of the door. Demetri's request for alternate flight information was met with a smiling stewardess telling him it would be only a minute longer and to please remain in his seat.

Demetri watched the repairman from his seat in first class. After trying to close the door for the twentieth time, the Mensa mechanic decided to check the sensor. A quick test proved the sensor was bad, but this meant the mechanic had to get some replacement parts from the warehouse. It took so long Demetri assumed the warehouse was in Maryland.

There were eight seats in first class and Demetri's bodyguards took four of those. Even though they were in the seats around him, everyone kept to themselves. An open airplane was not the place to discuss delicate business matters. Especially when everyone around them were norms.

Finally the flight had taken off and Demetri was able to relax for awhile. That is until an hour into the flight when Demetri felt the plane bank and head north. When he called the stewardess and asked what was going on he was informed that a storm front was in their flight path and they were going to fly around.

Between the two delays, the flight was three hours late. What had started as a simple flight with plenty of time had now become a race for darkness. Demetri had about fifteen minutes before the sun came up.

Looking over his shoulder to make sure his bodyguards were keeping up with him, Demetri began to walk even faster. The walls and people he passed were a blur. He rushed forward and into the baggage claim area. Over by the door, Demetri spotted one of the operatives that he had sent a few weeks before to scope out LA.

"Derrick, have you got our car handy?" Demetri asked as he looked at his watch for the umpteenth time since he got off the plane.

"Yes, it's at the curb. Do you have any luggage we have to wait for?" Derrick said.

"No, and let's get going," said Demetri. He pushed through the doors and started down the walkway toward the curb. "Which one is ours?"

Derrick caught up to him and pointed to a black SUV with the back windows tinted so black they could have been painted opaque. "Right here, we'll be fine in here," Derrick said.

Demetri reached the vehicle and stopped. He looked up at the eastern sky. The light pink starting to show made him check his watch again. "You going to drive?" he asked Derrick.

"No, I have a driver. He's a norm. Let's get in, and we'll be fine," Derrick said.

Demetri climbed into the car and moved to the far corner of the rear seat. Derrick and the bodyguards tossed the carry-on bags into the back and climbed in. Demetri had been worried about the rising sun that he hadn't noticed the thick black plastic wall separating them from the front seats until Derrick rapped on it with his knuckles.

The SUV pulled away from the curb and into the early morning airport traffic. Demetri tried to calm down, but he still had to get into the hotel.

"Did you have to have the car custom-made?" Demetri asked.

"Not at all. It belongs to a car service that I've used from time to time," said Derrick.

Demetri looked around the insides of the SUV. Other than the large Plexiglas block it looked like any other SUV. "Why would a car service have this vehicle? Why not a limo?"

"I never thought about it," said Derrick. "I mean, this is Hollywood. Limos are a dime a dozen and everyone assumes they contain celebrities. But who looks twice at a family SUV with a normal looking guy driving? You didn't see it, but the tailgate has a Starfleet Academy bumper sticker, and Billy, that's the driver, looks like he hasn't shaved in three days."

"As long as he can drive and get us to the hotel fast, that's all I care about," said Demetri.

The windows were heavily tinted, but Demetri could see out as the light grew. Demetri remembered why he hated to travel away from his city. Even the best laid plans of vampires were at the mercy of the norms. He checked his watch again.

"How much further?" Demetri asked.

"We're on Sepulveda now," said Derrick as he peered through the dark glass. "Almost there."

True to Derrick's word, a couple of turns later and Demetri saw they were pulling into an Embassy Suites Hotel. There was a covered lobby drop off, but rather than stopping, the SUV drove down into the parking garage. The dark of the garage blocked any light from reaching into the back of the vehicle, but Demetri felt the tight one-eighty they took on the ramp.

The SUV stopped and Derrick stepped out. Demetri could see they were parked next to the elevator in the parking garage. Next to them was an old blue car with a parking boot clamped to the front wheel. The light was dim and the air smelled of half burned gasoline.

"We'll take the elevator up one flight to the lobby. There aren't any skylights, and the front desk doesn't get any light from when the front door is opened."

Demetri nodded as he stepped into the open elevator. His men had grabbed the bags and were following him. Derrick was the last to get in, having taken a moment to sign the driver's receipt.

The lobby was long, spreading out at least a hundred yards away from the open elevator. As Demetri walked toward the front desk he saw there was more behind the bank of elevators as well. The hotel was four-stories high and the lobby ceiling went all the way up. Each floor was open to the lobby and Demetri could see businessmen tugging rolling suitcases along the open corridors.

Checking in was routine. Demetri and his now five men were in a block of suites on the second floor. Following the desk clerk's finger pointing and verbal instructions, Demetri lead the others up a staircase in the lobby to the second level. As he walked toward his room he saw the morning breakfast/evening lounge area where the clerk had said he could get a free breakfast. Cooks were busy prepping the area and a few norms were huddled over eggs and hash browns while they read the morning paper.

Demetri had everyone drop their stuff in their rooms and meet him at his suite. Two minutes later they were gathered in the front room.

"Okay, not a fun trip but we made it," said Demetri.

"I'd rather not have it that close again," said one of the bodyguards.

"To be honest, I've had closer," said Demetri, "but it's not a record I want to try breaking."

Everyone around him nodded in agreement. "Okay, the plan is for us to meet with the local boss, Dafyd Peack. He seems to run a loose organization, and I'm sure I can convince him of my story, that we are looking for Lucrecia."

"But she's dead," said Derrick.

"I know that, and you know that, but Peack doesn't know that we know that," said Demetri. "As far as he knows she is the reason I'm here."

He paused to make sure he had everyone's attention. "But the real reason we are here is Khalida Raven."

Everyone sat up a little straighter. They looked at each other as if trying to see if they heard correctly. Demetri was satisfied to see even Derrick, who had been so smug up until that point, was surprised.

"She's here?" Derrick asked.

"Yes. Based on a clue Lucrecia left I was able to track her down. Tonight we're going to take in a show, and pick her up. If all goes well we'll have her in our care before I meet Peack," said Demetri.

"How will you get her back to New York?" asked Derrick.

Demetri looked at Derrick. He was not used to having his plans questioned by such a junior level member of his organization. Demetri had not bothered to tell his bodyguards or Derrick that he had others coming in that night.

"I have a plan," said Demetri in a very even tone

while staring into Derrick's eyes.

Derrick must have taken the hint because he dropped his gaze from Demetri's.

"Is there anything I can do to help?" asked Derrick.

"For starters, tonight you can help us find our way around town without having to keep looking at maps," said Demetri.

"Can do. Where are you planning on going?" asked Derrick.

"Our first stop is a place called The Club. It's apparently a very hot night spot for the Goth crowd," said Demetri.

"I know the place," said Derrick. "Do you want me to get a car and driver to pick us up, or do you want to take cabs."

Demetri turned to him. "Think Derrick. If we take Khalida captive are we going to hail a cab? What would a human driver say if we dragged a woman kicking and screaming into the back of a limo think?"

"Uh," was all Derrick could get out.

"Exactly," said Demetri. "I want you to rent a panel van, something dark with no windows in the back. I want you to plan on driving it, because I don't want anyone I don't know involved."

"Anything else?" Derrick asked, his tone was enough to let Demetri know he was worried.

"Yes. I want you to make sure you know all the roads and alleys around The Club as well as all ways to and from Dafyd Peack's place. You know where it's at?"

Derrick nodded. "Yes, I know where it is, but I've never actually been there."

"Sloppy Derrick," said Demetri. "You didn't have to

go in, but you should have at least driven by. I guess you'll just have to study the maps and hope they are up to date."

Demetri looked around at the others, there was no look of question in any eyes. He had chosen his bodyguards for this mission well, and he had browbeaten Derrick into submission. He decided that Derrick had been experiencing too much freedom living in the field. When he was done in LA he would take Derrick back to New York. It was time for some re-indoctrination.

CHAPTER FOURTEEN

Vic put two large magnetic signs on the sides of the van, advertising a home security company. Where he'd gotten the signs, Jim had no idea. Vic also took off the license plate. He pulled out a new one he said he had taken off a junked car. Vic also pulled out a frame for it, a flat steel one that looked like one of those tribal tattoos that Jim had seen around the biceps of some hot chicks in the clubs. Vic said it was to distract people from looking too hard at the plate. In the slowly increasing light of day the van looked different. The signs covered the rust spots and the worst of the gray primer that dotted the van. No one had ever gotten around to doing the repainting that it so desperately needed.

Usually by standing at just the right angle to the side of the van, it was obvious that at some time it had been in a sidewise collision. The signs covered all that.

Jim's contribution to the cause was to stand holding a stack of light coveralls—also branded on the back with the home security company's logo—while each of the other seven men pulled one off the top, Vic, Ekson, Matt, Mike, Pete, Stevo, and Truck. Jim took one for himself, leaving three still in the stack. Ken and Woo had to work today, and no one had seen Lewis since the night before. Jim guessed he was probably at work also.

The coveralls were one-size fits all, which meant that Truck's coveralls strained at the seams, and Matt's floated around his body and flapped past his hands and feet. They rolled up Matt's sleeves and pant legs, and belted his coveralls around his waist. Which, in Jim's opinion, wasn't that much of an improvement, but no one asked so he kept it to himself. Matt wasn't the only one with rolled up sleeves and pants, but his were the most obvious.

"Look at the front of your coveralls," Vic instructed them, "See what your name is. Then we'll try to memorize everyone else's name."

Jim looked at his chest. There, neatly screen-printed, was a smaller version of the home security logo with the name "Smith" printed underneath.

Vic pulled out a clipboard. "All right, we'll call off. Jones?"

After a moment's pause, Mike said, "I'm Jones?"

"Just say 'here,'" Vic said.

He went through an entire list of seemingly ordinary names. Mike was to be Mr. Jones. Ekson was Mr. Brown. Jim was Mr. Smith, Matt was Mr. Anderson, Vic was Mr. Washington, Pete was Mr. Jackson, Stevo was Mr. Miller, and Truck was Mr. Johnson.

Knowing he'd have a hard time keeping all this straight, Jim tentatively raised his hand. "What if we forget?"

"If you forget just call out a "T" first name, like Todd," Vic said setting his clipboard aside. "If anyone gets too nosy, we'll can make up an excuse, like it's your first day. Or you usually work with another team."

"Or you're stupid." Truck pointed at Jim and laughed.

"All right." Vic picked up a stack of paper forms. "These are your instructions, read over them quickly now, except for the first two pages, which are camouflage. You can refer to them as you need to when we get there. We'll be divided into three groups. Your group is designated at the top. We're going to set up our vampire booby trap using fiber optics. It should allow us to take out all the vampires in the building, without harming the house itself. What we're going to tell them, and all of you leave the talking to me, is that we're upgrading their home security system. Any questions?"

They all piled into the van.

As Vic drove the van, Jim began to have serious doubts about their plan. What homeowner would let a bunch of strangers into their house to "upgrade" their security system? Even assuming Vic had gotten the information for his signs and coveralls from the actual security company the house's owner used, a simple phone call to the security company would reveal the truth. This plan really and truly depended on the vampires being either incredibly stupid, or incredibly disorganized.

Finally Jim could stand it no longer. "I don't think this plan is going to work. If we're not their security company—"

"We are," Vic said.

"If they call—"

"They won't." Vic glanced back at Jim. "Don't worry."

"Would you trust a bunch of strangers showing up unexpectedly at your house? To 'upgrade' your security system?" Jim looked around. Only Mike looked the least concerned.

"You worry too much." Vic sounded scornful. "They're only vampires. They'll be tired at this time of day. They won't be thinking straight, they'll be thinking of getting to bed. Trust me."

"Jim has a point," Mike said.

"You mean Smith has a point," Stevo said.

"Guys!" Vic shouted. "Don't worry about it. I've got it covered. And whatever you do, don't look nervous while you're there."

Sighing, Jim dropped it and looked out the window at the city. They were driving through some very nice areas. Jim realized he'd never been to any of the LA tourist attractions. Never been down Rodeo. Never been to any of the movie studios, or Disneyland. Most of what he'd seen in LA were the seedier areas at night. Back alleys and a few clubs, not the exclusive sort, that's all he had to show for a year and a half in the city.

His sister, Tracey, had always wanted to come here. She'd secretly hoped to be "discovered." Mostly, Jim knew this for certain, she'd wanted to get out of her small-town nobody-dom. That had been his dream, too, ever so long ago. Before his life had turned into a nightmare of death and squalor.

"Here we are," Vic announced.

Jim hurriedly checked his set of instructions. He was on the runner team, headed by Ekson. Their main job was to step and fetch for Vic's fiber optics team and Matt's control board team.

After parking, Vic turned back to look at everyone. "Okay now. Don't worry. I'll talk us in, and give you the signal. Everyone sit tight here."

As they watched Vic head for the door, Matt whispered, "The reason Vic knows this will work, and how to talk our way in, is that Vic does work for this company. Part time." Matt looked at Jim. "So don't worry."

The ten minutes they spent waiting for Vic felt like ten years to Jim. However, Vic finally gave them the signal, and everyone piled out.

"You three," Vic pointed at Ekson, Mike, and Jim, "Get the fiber optic rolls, and put one roll at every corner of the house." He patted Matt on the shoulder. "There's a woman just inside the door, she'll show you where the control box is."

Matt picked up a large cardboard box, and headed toward the front door. Pete grabbed a toolbox and followed him. Vic, Stevo, and Truck began putting on tool belts.

Ekson picked up a large spool, wrapped in a clear plastic film. Mike and Jim each reached for a similar spool.

The spools were heavier than Jim had expected. He was huffing and puffing by the time he reached the first corner of the house. Of course, Ekson had already claimed that spot for his spool.

Since the house was an old Victorian it had more than four corners. Ekson, Mike, and Jim stood around in that spot figuring out how many corners there were, and who would carry the spools to each one.

"This way we won't all try for the same corner," Ekson said.

Yet, somehow, it seemed to Jim that he got all the corners at the back of the house, while Ekson and Mike split the front and sides between them.

"Yes, yes," said Mike as they met at the van to get their next spool. "But you have less corners than we do."

"That's supposed to make it fair?" Jim asked.

Mike just walked off with his spool.

After placing the next spool, Jim heard Matt shout, "Smith!"

Remembering that was supposed to be his name, he responded with, "Where are you?"

"Inside."

Right next to where Jim was placing his spool was good-sized porch and a back door. Jim guessed that in the old days this would have been the tradesmen and servants' entrance. He had to let his eyes adjust to the gloomy darkness after stepped into the house. He could see that the room had been changed into a very functional mud room, complete with a large laundry sink, a couple rows of boots on shelves, and a few jackets hanging on hooks.

"Little more inside." Matt's voice drifted from one of two doorways that led deeper into the house.

Tentatively Jim peered into the next room. A bright spotlight in the corner cast gloomy shadows through the rest of the room. Ducts and pipes and wires lead to and from large squat hulking boxes, next to a series of hot water heaters. Jim guessed the rest of the large boxy equipment was air-conditioning and either a humidifier or a dehumidifier. He'd never learned how to tell one from the other, and was particularly amused by houses that had both.

In the corner, under the spotlight stood Matt and Pete. To their right was a window, painted over black, and possibly painted shut. To their left was a box on the wall that Jim recognized as a fuse box. On the wall behind Matt and Pete was another electrical box. Jim guessed it was the control box for the security system, but only because it looked like someone had taken it half apart, leaving wires dangling with bits attached.

"You need something?" Jim asked.

"There are four cardboard boxes under the middle seat of the van," Matt said. "Bring us the one labeled JOB-X5S."

Nodding, Jim retreated. Mike and Ekson complained that he wasn't getting his job done, and he explained about Matt's request. He found the boxes and headed to the back of the house.

Since he knew where he was going, Jim didn't bother waiting until his eyes adjusted to the darkness after he entered the house. Unfortunately there was a woman peeking into the room he was heading for, and he ran right into her.

Jim almost dropped the box, and nearly fell down himself. The woman glared at him, but didn't seem to be hurt.

"I'm so sorry," Jim said as he righted himself. "I didn't see you there. I didn't wait for my eyes to adjust after coming in. I'm really, really sorry."

The woman just looked at him strangely.

"Are you all right? I didn't hurt you did I? I'm so sorry," Jim said, hoping he'd find the right combination of words to get her to forgive him and go away. Or at least go away and not be mad at him.

"I'm fine," she said.

Well, that much was true. Now that his eyes had adjusted, Jim could see that she was a very good-looking woman. Her dark hair set off her pale skin and vivid blue eyes. Even here in the semi-darkness he could see the color of her eyes. She was rounded without being fat, and he'd almost run her down.

She was doing her own assessment of him, ending with a smile that didn't reveal her teeth. "So, do you like clubbing?"

The mention of nightclubs reminded him that this was a vampire. Perhaps one he'd missed at the club. He tried to think fast. "Ah, no ma'am. They serve liquor there, and you know liquor is the devil's brew. I wouldn't let the devil's brew touch these lips."

She leaned over the box he was carrying, and ran the tip of her finger over his lips. "No, we wouldn't want that."

"But, but..." His mind didn't seem to be thinking fast enough. Maybe she wasn't a vampire. Maybe she'd like to go out with him. Maybe he should test this theory first, before he slobbered all over her. "The church is having a picnic next Saturday afternoon. Would you like go with me?"

Shaking with repressed laughter, she said, "Why, you don't even know my name."

"Oh lover boy," Pete sing-songed from the next room. "Quit trying to pick up girls for your next church social, and get in here and work."

"Sorry," Jim said one last time to the woman as he fled into the other room. It was really too bad she was a vampire, but he hadn't been to church since he didn't know when, and had no social to take her to anyway.

Pete mock hit his head as he entered. Matt settled for grabbing the box, sending Jim away.

The vampire woman had disappeared, when Jim left.

Ekson and Mike had finished placing their spools, left the rest for Jim, and disappeared somewhere. He picked up the load, and hefted it to the back of the house.

Mike and Ekson were holding a ladder at the back of the house while Truck climbed up, unraveling the spool of fiber optic cable behind him. Vic fed the end of the cable into a hole in the wall of the house near the black-painted window of the utility room. The spool itself remained at the base of the ladder, with the cable lengthening in a loop between the spool, Truck, and the hole.

"Hurry it up," Vic said to Jim.

It was a hot day, and the coveralls over his regular clothes made Jim even hotter. As the day progressed they ran fiber optic cable under all the rain gutters on the house, feeding them into various spots in the attic and crawl spaces under the roofs.

They tried to be as quiet and unobtrusive as it was possible to be when they were climbing ladders, drilling holes, and slithering through crawl spaces, but their work obviously bothered the many people in the house.

At one point, Jim overheard Vic say to a complainer, "Sorry to disturb you, sir. Just think how much worse this would be if we tried to do it at night, when everyone was sleeping."

Remembering that Matt had said that wiring houses for security was Vic's part time job, Jim felt sorry for him. This was hot, tedious, laborious work. It made Jim's checkout clerking seem simple and effortless.

"Last bit of cable." Vic gave one end to Jim. "Go under the house into the crawl space; Mike's there, he'll show you where he drilled the last hole."

The coolness under the house made up for the cramped crawling. He found Mike by moving toward the only light which came from Mike's flashlight.

Mike pointed tiredly to the hole, and indicated that Jim should start feeding the cable in and just keep feeding it. They were both too tired to talk.

"Did you find out where he is?"

It took a moment for Jim to realize the voice came from above them in the house. A bit of duct work protruded from the floor above them heading off to the utility room.

"The Embassy Suites in El Segundo." The voice chuckled. "Near the airport, huh. He must have been cutting it close. Do you have a room number?" A pause. "201. Got it. How many vampires did he bring with him?"

Jim wondered if his eyes were as big as Mike's, as they stared at each other. Suddenly the cool crawl space was a little too cold and a little too cramped. The adrenaline pumping through Jim's body made him want to jump up and run away.

"Only four? You're right, he's got to have a strike force waiting for his word to fly in." Another pause. "Still, if we can get him while he's only got four with him, the strike force will never arrive."

Realizing he'd stopped breathing and feeding cable, Jim forced himself to breath quietly through his accommodatingly open mouth. He began feeding the cable through again, very slowly and very quietly.

"Well, we're ready for him here. He hasn't contacted us yet, but I'm sure he'll get around to it. Knowing Demetri Vasile he'll want to scope things out a bit, and see if he can annoy us before he confronts us." This pause didn't last very long. "Keep in touch."

Jim waited for a few moments, but there was nothing more to hear. Mike signaled to him to stop feeding the cable, and they both crawled out.

Vic was waiting by the van when Jim and Mike got there. "Next we install the new alarm lights. Jim, you don't..."

"Vic, we overheard something," Mike said. He jumped into the van. Vic, Truck, and Stevo followed him. Jim waited outside the door to make certain their conversation wasn't interrupted and wasn't overheard.

"We'll finish this job here, then scout this other problem," Vic said to Jim by way of explanation. He pointed to Jim. "Don't even try to install any light fixtures. We'll be doing that. You just bring us the boxes as we need them."

They systematically replaced all the alarm lights in the house. Each room and hallway had a light fixture to provide an alert, both by sound and by light, and, since the system had its own emergency generator, to light the way through the house should the electricity go out.

It was nearing five when they finally finished up. Everyone was exhausted, and Jim expected that Vic would hold off springing the booby trap until they could all catch some rest.

On the drive home Vic said, "It's not bad enough we've got our own vampires, now we've got them flying in from out of state."

Truck chuckled. "Well they have to come from somewhere."

Vic spared him a quick glare. "We'll get back to those

vampires in the house we just rigged after we take care of this new this new one."

"When are we going to do that?" Truck asked.

"Jim and Mike and Woo can head over to the Embassy Suites, find this Demetri Vasile, and do a stake out, as it were, until we can get everyone else together," Vic said.

"Woo is at work," Mike said.

"And I have to be at work by six," Jim said, wondering if he'd have the energy to do anything. He'd already put in a full eight hours. "Thank goodness it's only a short shift."

"When'll you be done?" Vic asked.

"Nine."

"All right. New plan. Mike, Pete, and Stevo locate and follow our new quarry. We meet up at nine-thirty. Get rid of Demetri Vasile and these other vampires he brought with him. Then about midnight we'll go spring our booby trap on that houseful. After tonight, LA will be a much better place."

Everyone in the van agreed with him.

Later at work, Jim wondered if it really would be. No matter how many vampires they killed there were always more. Now they were flying in from out of state.

He was so tired from his long day of work, and the thought of what they had planned for tonight, that Jim missed scanning several items from a customer's purchase. The customer didn't seem to mind, and smirked irritatingly as Jim's boss chewed Jim out.

Jim tried to keep his mind on what he was doing after that, but still his thoughts kept wandering. The few vampires he'd seen today had all looked and acted like ordinary people. The one vampire woman acted as if she liked him, though Jim suspected she was merely amusing herself.

From the conversation he'd overheard, it appeared that Demetri Vasile was some kind of rival to the vampires in the house they booby trapped. Jim had never thought of vampires having rivals. What would they be rivals over?

The only thing vampires really needed was blood, and there were far more ordinary people in the world than there were vampires. So why bother fighting when there was more than you could ever use walking all around you?

It reminded him of when he'd helped babysit his bratty cousins. Their parents had made certain both boys had exactly the same toys, same clothes, same furniture, same everything. Yet those two fought each other more than any one else Jim had ever met.

Jim wished they'd never captured and held Lucrecia. He wished they'd never booby-trapped the vampire house. He wished that things were as they were before, when Matt's inventions didn't work. When he just staked vampires the minute he was certain they were vampires. Back when no vampire had any name that he knew. Back when they were ugly monsters lurking in the dark to prey on innocents.

When he was certain of what was right and what he had to do.

Back when vampires didn't seem so human.

CHAPTER FIFTEEN

Normally, Raven enjoyed walking to the club from her home at a leisurely pace. Tonight she would have preferred to get a ride, but Cowboy had to go by his job site as soon as the sun went down. He promised to come by before the end of her second set and take her out for a drive. Her second option was the bus, but that required her to travel out of her way and transfer twice. Unless it was raining it was easier, and faster, to walk.

Tonight however, she didn't take an easy pace. She kept her focus on the sidewalk ahead of her and walked fast. It was a good thing she was a vampire. Had she been human she would have certainly been huffing and puffing after the first half mile. She decided she was going to have to take Cowboy's suggestion and get a prepaid cell phone. She could have called Tina or Clarisa for a ride if she had been able to call them before sundown. That was the problem of relying on an old payphone at the corner store, she couldn't always use it when she needed.

As she passed the spot where she had been attacked the other night, she looked over where she had left her attacker. Dark spots stained the sidewalk. They could be blood, or urine. It was hard to tell in the dim light of the street light. She kept walking and soon was in sight of the club.

There was at least an hour before the show was due to start but already there was a good-sized crowd. Raven hoped it was that word had gotten around about the show the night before. It made her smile. Raven was enjoying her life for the first time in too many years. She only hoped it could continue.

She hoped Cowboy was right, and she could trust Dafyd. It was refreshing to hear that he didn't put any more stock in the so-called prophecy than she did. She had been so afraid he would take one look at her and clamp chains on her and lock her away. That was the fate that awaited her with Demetri.

When Dafyd had told her that he already knew she was living in the area, but had never approached her, she started to trust him. He could have tried to grab her at any time. If she had to live in a city with organized vampires, she much preferred to live in LA with Dafyd's hands off approach.

Raven stepped into the club. She saw Charlie talking to the barman. He looked up, and she nodded when she caught his eye. He gave her a slight wave and went back to his conversation. Probably telling the poor guy to water down the drinks even more.

She stood to the side of the doorway, looking over the crowd. If Raven could catch Tina and Clarisa early enough before the show, she wanted to share some ideas she had for changing the mix a bit. The rush of the other night was so incredible she wanted to do it again.

There were a lot of regulars as well as a bunch she hadn't seen before. She didn't see either Tina or Clarisa. It was too early for them to be backstage, more likely they hadn't arrived yet. Raven started to head toward the door to the back to see if she was wrong, when she stopped in mid step. She felt a chill run up her spine, and she quickly stepped back into the shadows near the door.

She wasn't sure what she had seen that made her stop, but something had ignited her instinct to blend into the furniture and hide. Raven looked over the room again, this time going slower, examining each person closer whether she had seen them before or not. A man sitting at a table about halfway across the room with his back to her looked familiar. Something about his hair, his ears, the way he sat.

Ice formed in the pit of her stomach and was replaced with the feeling of lava running through her body. It was hard to be sure without seeing his face, and if she saw his face then he could see hers, but Raven knew that it was Demetri. She watched the back of his head intently, afraid he would turn but wanting him to so she would know for sure.

As she watched, the man began to turn his head. Raven caught a glimpse of his jaw line before turning and bolting out of the club and into the crowd hanging around outside. She started to run away, racing down the street and around the corner, but stopped as she went by the alley.

She was pretty sure it was Demetri, but not absolutely sure. And if it was him she was sure she got out before he saw her. But she was on foot. How far could she get if it was him and he did see her? Raven had to beat back her flight reflex and turn down the alley. She moved through the shadows, keeping quiet while moving as fast as she could. When she got to the stage door Raven knocked, and then cringed at the echo the sound made.

Raven turned around and watched the alley for signs that someone had followed her. She felt the door bump against her back as Manny opened it.

"Hi, Raven," said Manny.

"Hi, Manny. Sorry to bother you but I need to get in without being seen," said Raven.

"What's going on?"

"Well, I thought I saw someone in the club that I don't want to see," said Raven.

"You want me to get rid of him? I can toss him out. Which one is he," said Manny as he closed the alley door and started to move toward the front of the club.

"No, Manny, wait. He's not a nice guy and I don't want you to get hurt," said Raven. "Besides, I'm not sure if it's him or not. I'm going to go and peek through the peep hole, and see if I can get a better look at him."

Raven hadn't realized it until she said it to Manny, but she needed to know if it really was Demetri. The best way was to look at the face of the man she saw sitting at the table. There was a small hole in the wall from the backstage that was used to check out a crowd before going on. She pulled the cloth out that stopped it up and peered through.

Raven could see the table where the man had been sitting, but there was no one sitting there now. She twisted and strained to see more of the club, but she could only see the main part. There was a lot to the corners and sides that she couldn't see.

She should have kept going she thought. If she had kept going she could have gotten away. Now she felt trapped. Was it Demetri? Did he see her? If he saw her, did he follow her? Raven started to get dizzy just thinking about the problem. Cowboy, she needed to get a hold of Cowboy.

"Manny, can I borrow your cell phone?" Raven asked.

"Sure," said Manny as he handed her his phone. "Is it the guy?"

"I don't know. The person who I saw isn't there anymore."

Raven punched in Cowboy's number. She felt antsy waiting for him to answer. When her call was answered it wasn't Cowboy, it was his voicemail.

"Cowboy, please help. It's Demetri, and he's at the club. I'm going to try and get to Dafyd's."

"Thanks," Raven said as she handed the phone back to Manny.

Manny took the phone and slipped it back in his pocket. "You need to get out of here?"

"If possible. I just don't want to be seen by that guy if it's who I think it is," said Raven.

"You can borrow my car," said Manny. "It's parked right in front, second spot to the right of the front door."

"Thanks, Manny, but I don't know how to get to your car. He's not in the seat I saw him in. He could be somewhere in the club, or he might be in the alley if he saw me and followed."

Manny reached for a coat hanging on a nail. "Here, take my coat and hat. Tuck your hair in and keep your head down. My car is the blue Honda. If you can at least get ahead of him you have a chance to get away."

Raven accepted the coat. She didn't know what to say. "Thanks, Manny. This means a lot to me."

Wrapping herself into the coat, letting it fall loose around her body, Raven tucked her hair up into the black Highlander baseball cap Manny had given her. She went to the door that led from backstage to the front of the club. Clutching Manny's car keys she opened the door and slipped out in what she hoped was an unobtrusive way.

No one paid her any attention and Raven had a chance to look around the club. No Demetri. That didn't mean it wasn't him, but at least she could get through the club without being stopped.

At the door Raven paused again to see if Demetri might be outside. Not a sign of him. She saw Manny's Honda and rushed for it. After a slight fumble of her keys Raven was inside and the engine roared to life. Forgetting to look for oncoming traffic Raven pulled out and headed for Dafyd Peack's mansion.

She thought about not going to see Dafyd. She hadn't gotten a good look at the guy in the club. But where had he gone. Others that had been in the club when she stepped in were still there. There could be a lot of reasons why he was no longer at the table. Still, Raven had survived a long time by trusting her instincts.

It only took seconds for Raven to decide that her best course of action was to go to Dafyd. Perhaps he had some news that would confirm that the man she saw was Demetri. If she had trouble getting a hold of Cowboy, maybe he did too.

Raven downshifted as she went around a corner, and then sped up again. Raven followed the same route Cowboy had taken when they had been to Dafyd's before. She raced along the streets, ignoring the speed limit and sailing through intersections on yellow lights.

Sooner than she expected, but longer than she wanted, Raven pulled into the driveway of Dafyd's mansion. She pulled in beside his house in the long, wide driveway in front of the detached garage, and parked in the empty spot closest to the house. Looking around, worrying for the first time that she might have been followed, Raven tossed Manny's hat and coat in his car. She ran for the door and rang the bell. She tried to catch her breath and calm herself while she waited for someone to answer.

CHAPTER SIXTEEN

Demetri felt himself relax as he sat watching the children play at The Club. Hairstyles and clothing may come and go, and even come back again, but there will always be those who look to be on the outside of society. The Goths were part of the current incarnation of the fringe society. Before them there had been the punks, further back, the beatniks, circus performers, and gypsies. An ever-changing group who lived off the mystique of living on the fringe, the unknown, the sharp edge of society that could cut and sometimes kill.

Watching the people moving about the club, Demetri sipped a glass of scotch, enjoying the smoky taste in his mouth. It didn't have the same effect on him that it did before he became godlike when compared to the norms around him, but he still enjoyed the aroma, the taste, the feel as it slid down his throat.

It had been a long time since Demetri could sit in a club and not be recognized. He was glad he had decided to leave his crew in the van. His reasoning was that Khalida was more likely to spot a large group. Even though they were all vampires they would stand out in this club. He had also forgone his usual business suit and instead was wearing an outfit of black denim and leather. He wanted to blend. The plus side was he could sit, relax, and enjoy the pastime of people watching.

Demetri had lived long enough that he could predict behavior from the subtlest clues. A flick of an eye in one direction, the flare of nostrils, breathing patterns, and a dozen other tells that Demetri used to divine not a person's motivation, but their desires. It was a skill he had applied to his business quite successfully. Vampires liked to think they were mysterious and hard to read, but their desires were sometimes more obvious than a norm's.

The young man Demetri had been watching was finally making his move. Demetri had observed him sneaking glances at a group of women. Based on when he looked and his reaction to them Demetri had placed a bet with himself as to who was the target of his affection. Or lust. The youth mooned like a romantic poet, but Demetri also caught glimpses of pure lust and primal desire. When the young man finally had gathered his courage and approached the young women Demetri had won his bet. Lust had won out and the boy sought out the dark-haired beauty with the greatest amount of cleavage showing.

Demetri took another drink and began to look around the club for another subject. There was still an hour before the band was scheduled to play, but he wanted to be in place before the show started.

As he turned, some motion caught Demetri's attention out of the corner of his eye. He turned all the way around to face the door. The door was open and people were coming in and going out. Two men that seemed to have a competition to see who could cover more of their body with tattoos were walking in. One was looking back over his shoulder at someone outside. Demetri shifted to see what he was looking at. It was a woman, nice backside, short, deep red hair. Khalida.

Demetri rose and started for the door.

"Hey, five bucks," said the waitress. She came to block his way to the door, holding her serving tray so she could use it as a shield or a weapon.

Demetri fumbled in his pockets and tossed a twenty at her before pushing past and running out the door. When he got to the curb outside the club he couldn't see any sign of the redheaded woman. There were a lot of partygoers hanging around, milling about, and getting in his way. He tried to see around and over them, but without any luck.

If it was Khalida she might have seen him and that was why she left. The woman had not been any farther in the club than the door, or Demetri would have noticed her. Hoping his people in the van would spot Khalida and stop her if she went that way, Demetri moved down the sidewalk the other direction.

There was an alley at the end of the building. Demetri looked down the alley but couldn't see anything distinctive. The ground had random pieces of garbage and two dumpsters along the wall. He looked back down the street the way he had come, but still saw no sign of Khalida. The crowd was much thinner around the alley and he couldn't see her down the street. The alley was his best bet.

It was possible that she had a car parked behind the club, or had run down there to work her way to the other streets around the club. Demetri set off down the alley. He tried to move as fast as possible while keeping quiet. If Khalida was hiding behind the dumpsters or around the corner, he didn't want to lose the element of surprise.

Demetri reached the end of the building without seeing any sign of her. He continued around the corner toward a cross street, hoping she had run this way. He had moved a dozen yards when three humans stepped out to block his way. He knew they were humans by the smell of their breaths, the heavy smell of grilled meat was easily picked up by his nose.

They held themselves with confidence. They were either accomplished thugs, or worse. There was no clamoring and egging on between them, no attempts to try and get another to attack first.

"Pretty far from home, aren't you," said one of the norms.

Demetri started to step back away from them. He wasn't exactly sure what the norm meant. It would be next to impossible for any norms to know who he was and that he wasn't local. He took another step when he heard a shuffled step behind him.

Shifting his position so he could see who was behind him without letting the three in front of him completely out of his sight. Four more were blocking his retreat.

"We've got enough of your kind around here to deal with, we don't need to import any more," said the norm that was speaking for the group.

It was worse. Demetri read the tells. The confident stance, coming in a good sized group, and knowing that he was a vampire from out of town led Demetri to conclude that he had stumbled into a gang of vampire hunters. It wasn't the first time, and Demetri was determined that it wasn't going to be the last.

"You've got me confused with someone else," said Demetri. "I'm just trying to get back to where I parked my car."

"Your van is in the other direction," said the norm.

He had been in town less than a day and these hunters had picked up his tracks. Someone had to have tipped them off, but who? His first thought was that Dafyd was trying to get rid of him in a way that he could blame a band of hunters. Demetri would need more information, but first he had to get out of the alley alive.

The others had spread out as best they could behind and in front of him. He still had the sides of the alley to work with, and there were so many of them that they were still a bit clumped up. They all seemed to have stakes for weapons. One of the norms behind him had some sort of gun, but it had wires sticking out of it. He was focused on his gun, moving things on it, and not paying attention.

Feint at strength and attack at weakness. Demetri leapt toward the three that had originally blocked him. They stepped back, but did not drop their defensive posture. Before they could move forward to reclaim the ground they had given to him, Demetri spun and rushed the four behind him.

As he expected, three of the four backed up, maintaining a defensive stance, stakes out and at the ready. The forth norm was caught unaware, still trying to adjust his gun. Demetri grabbed the norm around his arms, forcing the gun to fall to the ground.

"Matt, no," shouted the spokesman.

One of the four rushed Demetri, wooden stake raised to strike. Demetri spun around so his victim became a shield. As the attacker slowed in his rush, Demetri spun around again and kicked him in the gut sending the stake clattering to the ground and the attacker into the wall. Demetri watched long enough to be sure he crumpled to the ground.

"Let him go," said the speaker.

"All in good time," said Demetri.

Demetri held his captive with his left arm tight around his chest, trapping his arms. As hard as the norm struggled he was no match for Demetri's strength. This left his right arm free to fight. He backed against one of the walls, taking in all of his attackers. Gripping his captive by the hair, he yanked his head to the side, baring his neck. Demetri let them see his fangs poised above neck before speaking.

"I didn't come here for trouble with you. All of you move down that alley," Demetri said, using his shaking head to indicate the alley away from the club.

No one moved. Demetri said, "Do it or I'll feed." He again bared his fangs over the neck of his captive.

"Do what he says," said the voice of the group. "We've got to get Matt back."

Demetri watched carefully as two helped their wounded companion join the other three. Demetri shifted so he was walking backwards away from the group, his struggling captive actually helping him to move away. The hunters stepped forward, keeping pace.

"Back off a bit or I bite," said Demetri, baring his fangs over flesh for effect again.

This time when Demetri stepped back, the others didn't follow. He carefully stepped back a few more paces and when he had a comfortable space between him and them, Demetri pulled out his cell phone.

"Meet me at the mouth of the alley on the west side of the club as fast as you can," he said when Derrick answered.

The hunters started to move forward again. "Just let him go. We won't follow you," said the norm.

"Not just yet," said Demetri. "I think I like his company, and we'll just stroll back up the alley together. Don't do anything stupid and I'll let him go."

Demetri had made his way back down the alley along the club. He could hear a vehicle stop at the end of the alley. He chanced a look over his shoulder and was relieved to see it was his guys.

"Who sent you to kill me?" Demetri asked.

"No one sent us, we tracked you down," said the voice.

"Right," said Demetri. "I might believe you if I had been in town longer, and you obviously know details about me, so who tipped you off?"

"Let Matt go, and I'll tell you."

Demetri shook his head as he continued to drag Matt toward his van. "It doesn't work like that."

Demetri had reached the alley mouth, the van a couple of feet away. One of his guards had opened the door and started to get out, but Demetri motioned him to stay inside.

"Last chance," Demetri said.

"No one told us," said the voice.

"Now you're being stupid," said Demetri.

Demetri yanked Matt's head to one side and sunk his teeth into the soft yielding flesh. Blood spurted into his mouth, the heat and taste pushing him toward a frenzy. Vaguely aware of the vampire hunters hesitatingly rushing him, Demetri stumbled back across the sidewalk still using the limp body as a shield. Unable to look behind him to find the van's door, Demetri took several tries to get the dead weight of Matt's unconscious body into the back of the van, while Matt's friends screamed in agony and tentatively attempted a rescue.

"Drive, drive," shouted Demetri as he climbed in and slammed the door.

The van shot out into traffic before Demetri got settled into a chair. Matt had passed out when Demetri's teeth had sunk into his flesh. Demetri leaned in, and again bit Matt's neck. This time Demetri sucked at the wound, the taste of hot blood better than any scotch ever made, the power it made him feel more intoxicating.

"There," said Demetri as he sat back. "That should be enough to turn him. When he is done transforming I'll get the answers I need."

Demetri looked out the front of the van. Derrick was driving, and seemed to be randomly taking turns.

"Where are you going?" Demetri asked.

"Nowhere right now, I mean we're driving but I'm not heading anywhere. You said drive so I did," said Derrick.

"Fine, fine," said Demetri. "Take us over to Peack's place."

"Uh, okay," said Derrick. He leaned over and looked out the front of the windshield, then out the side windows.

"Problem, Derrick?" Demetri asked, he tone telling those used to him that there had better not be a problem.

"No, it's just that we took off and I was making some random turns because I wasn't sure if anyone was going to try and follow us, well I'm not sure where we are right now."

Demetri shook his head in disbelief that he was relying on this person. "Find where you are and get to Peack's. Stop at a gas station if you have to."

While Derrick worked their way back into known territory Demetri bent over and watched Matt who lay on the floor between the front seats and middle bench of the van. It wasn't much longer until Matt's eyes fluttered open.

"I'm alive," he said.

"In a manner of speaking," said Demetri. "Your old friends might argue the point."

Matt blinked, looking up at Demetri. He pushed himself up from the floor, and sat in the seat next to Demetri.

"No," Matt said. "I feel so much more alive than before. Stronger, getting up was so easy, my body responded like fluid shifting to a new position. I feel like I could take on the entire football team from my old school single-handed, and kick some ass."

Demetri chuckled. "Yes, that's how most feel when they are converted. I hope you don't mind that I brought you over."

Matt was flexing his arms, stretching them out from his body, then pulling them back to examine his hands as if he had never seen them before. "No, not at all. I'm just sorry I didn't come over earlier. I'm Matt Mann by the way."

Demetri shook the offered hand. "Demetri."

They rode in silence for another minute. "Matt, do you feel up to answering a couple of questions for me?"

"Sure," said Matt.

"Well, I'm curious how you and your friends came to be in that alley tonight. It sounded like you were waiting for me, and I didn't tell anyone I was going to be there," said Demetri.

"Oh, that. Sorry about that. It's really kind of simple," said Matt.

Demetri sat and listened while Matt went through the entire story of the band of vampire hunters he was a part of, the inventions he worked to complete, and the giant trap that had been set up at the vampire mansion.

"So you figured out how to kill vampires with holy water and lasers? Impressive," said Demetri.

"Thanks, but right now I'm not feeling very proud of

that," said Matt. "It was while we were setting up the equipment for the trap that a couple of the guys heard you were coming in and where you were staying."

"Matt, you probably aren't aware of the fact that vampires have been forming rival organizations around the country. I've been trying to bring all of us together so we could work to establish ourselves in the world, and not have to skulk in the shadows anymore."

"Really, wow, I had no idea," said Matt.

"Well, that machine you described could really help expedite matters here in Los Angeles. It could save lots of time and the lives of your fellow vampires. Does that sound like something that would interest you?"

Matt looked at Demetri for a couple of minutes. Demetri let his take all the time he needed.

"That would be an even bigger, and more important cause than what I had done before," Matt said.

"Yes it would," said Demetri. "Matt, I want you to join my team. We take care of business here and then you go back to New York with me and become a part of my staff. I could use someone with your creativity and the technical knowledge behind it."

Matt stuck out his hand to Demetri. "Yes, I would love to join you."

Demetri shook Matt's hand while continuing. "Okay here's the plan. We're going to the mansion you wired for your trap. I have to go inside, and I'll take you with me, but after I leave I want you to set off your trap and get out."

"I can do that," said Matt. "It should kill all of the vampires in the house."

"Not vampires, Matt, dissidents. The enemy. By taking the lives of some we build a better order for vampires and humans alike."

"We're here," said Derrick from the front of the van.

CHAPTER SEVENTEEN

A crisis had arrived, and Dafyd's organization was working like the well-oiled machine he'd always hoped it would be. Everyone doing what they could for the greater good. No one was panicking; everyone was at their station, doing their job, dealing with this problem just like they'd deal with any other. Dafyd couldn't have been more pleased. They had the strength, stamina, and resilience to overcome this. Logic, foresight, and discipline should be all they needed to endure, to win the game.

But...

Dafyd couldn't get Raven out of his thoughts. He thought by now he'd overcome his youthful superstitions, his childlike belief in some higher power, in gods, great spirits, karma, and enlightenment. Enlightenment, ha, he'd yet to meet anyone that could see beyond their own skin, and that went double for "holy" men. Certainly all he'd been through for the past couple thousand years should have burned all that out of him.

But...

Prophecies, seers, wizards, Shamans. Lies, all lies. Logic and that wonderful invention, science, told him so. Guaranteed it. Proved it.

But...

He turned again in his bed, twisting the covers, trying vainly to rest. He had to rest. Tonight he would meet with Demetri Vasile, and Dafyd wanted to look rested and assured. Dafyd desperately wanted to put that striding megalomaniac in his place. Preferably in ashes six feet underground.

But...

If the prophecy of the crimson heir wasn't real, wasn't true, how could Raven meet its requirements? Dafyd had dismissed that particular prophecy years ago. He'd never met anyone that had changed that much simply on being turned into a vampire. Most vampires were stuck looking exactly like they had when they'd been turned—young, old, thin, fat, short, tall, balding, graying, wrinkled, even scars remained the same. Dafyd knew a few vampires that had managed to change the thin or fat ratio, and hair dyes were a wonderful invention. For vampires however, what you looked like before you were turned was what you looked like after you were turned.

But...

But, a little voice whispered in his mind that Demetri believes she is the crimson heir and Demetri turned her, so he would know what she looked like both before and after. No, Demetri didn't believe, Demetri knew.

Coincidence. It had to be coincidence. Strange

things always happened. How did that old saying go? Statistically all things are possible, just not probable. Science and logic could explain this. If Dafyd just put enough thought into it.

Vikings had landed in the Americas long before the English got there. So, maybe she'd inherited red hair from some odd old Viking ancestors she didn't know about. And what? She would have had red hair before she'd been turned.

Dafyd tossed again in bed. There had to be a solution. Maybe before she was turned she dyed her hair to match the rest of her tribe. She didn't want to look different. That was it.

So, how had it immediately turned red?

The old dyes weren't very good, they were always washing out. Except the ones that stained permanently.

Flinging back the covers, Dafyd slung his legs over the side of the bed and sat for a moment in the dark, rubbing his face. He thought about turning on his bedside light, but he didn't need it to see. And his habits had been set before there was electricity to provide instant light.

But...

Why should Demetri Vasile know of, have created, the answer to the prophecy? That megalomaniacal upstart, that overblown dictator. It was just so wrong, so unfair.

Unless Dafyd had it backwards.

If Vasile had created Raven then perhaps his megalomania stemmed from that incident, not the other way around.

That made sense.

Still, why Vasile? Why not Dafyd? Dafyd wondered what he would have done differently if it had been him. If he had been the one who knew who was the fulfillment of that prophecy.

Ah, said that little voice in his head, *but you do know who is the fulfillment of that prophecy.*

Dafyd stopped for a moment. It seemed that the whole world hesitated with him. That was the crux of the problem that had been destroying his rest all day. The game was about to change.

He knew. Dafyd knew the prophecy was real. He knew who was the crimson heir. He knew who was destined to unite and rule all vampires. To cap it all, the crimson heir had put herself within his sphere.

Under normal circumstances, this information would have been shared with all the team leaders in his organization. Oscar's analysts would have been all over it, while Dafyd and the other team leaders hashed out what to do about Raven.

Now, however, everything was in crisis. No one in the entire organization knew except Dafyd which seemed appropriate, since it was his organization. It suddenly occurred to him that with everyone spread out like this it would be harder for an outsider to attack and destroy them, but relatively simple for one team leader to grab the reins of their portion of the organization and destroy the rest. Or sheer off in a different direction, breaking away.

Something to think about, once Dafyd was ruling the world.

Having thought it, what had been up until so shortly

ago unthinkable, Dafyd found that his confusion and indecision lifted. He just needed to decide what the game was.

He would somehow coax Raven back here, bring her under his control, and then the world would be his for the plucking. Most likely Raven would come to him of her own accord.

Demetri Vasile would pay for his perfidy.

Dafyd smiled to himself, letting his fangs show, and turned the lights on in his room. Time to get ready for the night.

His room was comfortable, practical, and straightforward. He had a queen size sleigh bed, with only light blankets. Dark wood dressers, dark wood chair, dark wood dumb-valet, the carpet was a deep soft green, and the curtains blacked out all sunlight. Dafyd dressed quickly in the clothes he had laid out in the morning.

He'd gotten to bed late because of all the interruptions from the new security installation. From one standpoint it seemed an odd time for Petra to decide to upgrade their security, but from a different standpoint it made sense. He hadn't been able to get a hold of Petra when they'd first shown up, but the company confirmed that the one in charge was one of their employees. After that, Dafyd had forgotten to check back with Petra. They'd only bothered with the interior emergency lighting. Dafyd had thought about refusing them on the basis that no one in his organization needed interior lighting for any purpose other than convenience and to appear normal. However, it was that "appear normal" that convinced him. Normal people had such lights, and the original installation had included them, so they had to allow it to keep up appearances.

In the end, Dafyd had told them to go ahead. He'd had too many other problems to deal with to be bothered with petty foolishness. He'd take it up with Petra after this crisis was over.

Between, the security installation and Raven, he'd been unable to get a proper rest.

However, Dafyd felt fine. Energetic. Pumped. Now that he'd decided what to do about Raven, he no longer needed any rest. He just needed to get going.

Dafyd walked the house, checking to see who was up—only himself and Chuck his assistant manning the communications for headquarters.

"Anything to report?" Dafyd asked Chuck as he stepped into the communications room.

"No negative reports." Chuck pulled up a different screen on his computer. "All communication lines are up. Nothing new from Oscar's analysts. They haven't put up anything new on any other prophecies than what we already knew, and they haven't posted the locations of any seers since some doofus posted the Mormon prophet in Salt Lake City at nine this morning. I suspect Oscar gave them an earful, and told them to take it seriously." He ran the screen through a series of reports. "Everyone else is hunkered down where they're supposed to be, doing what they're supposed to do. So, nothing new."

Nodding, Dafyd said, "Carry on." He patted the pants pocket he kept his cell phone in. "Call me if there's anything important."

The rest of the house was quiet, and except for the bedrooms, uninhabited. Exactly as it should be at this hour of the day. Dafyd took himself up to his office to sort through whatever Oscar had sent to his computer.

The house came alive at sunset, and shortly after those members of Dafyd's headquarters team that didn't live in the house arrived.

At that point, he waited by the phone in the blue parlor with Chuck and a few others. Vasile would be calling soon, trying to sell Dafyd his lies. Dafyd had his own lies to give Demetri in return. How he loved the game.

Especially now that the stakes had just been raised.

Demetri Vasile called. Chuck answered the phone officiously, before handing it over to Dafyd. Of course they were recording the whole thing. Just in case.

"Demetri Vasile. It's been a long time since I heard your name," Dafyd said heartily into the phone. "So you vacationing in our beautiful city?"

"Something like that," Demetri said.

"Well, do try the Disney theme park. The night parades are not to be missed," Dafyd said. "Perhaps we could get together sometime."

After a few more hearty just-old-acquaintances-setting-up-a-reunion type exchanges, Demetri had an invitation to headquarters at about eleven-thirty that night.

Dafyd hung up the phone. "Welcome to my parlor, said the spider to the fly."

Chuck grinned. "We're ready for him."

"Got all the stakes sharpened?" Dafyd asked.

"And the knives." Dafyd's personal bodyguard, Vlad, patted his coat pocket. "Makes cutting his head off ever so much easier."

"Check the blood supply," Dafyd said. "We want only the best for our guest."

Nodding, Chuck said, "I'll see to it."

The waiting was getting to Dafyd. He wanted this over with. Killing Demetri would put Raven in his debt, and he wanted to get on with the game. But waiting was part of the game, so he tried to be patient.

Shortly after ten, Chuck brought Raven into the blue parlor.

"Welcome. This is rather unexpected," Dafyd said, motioning for her to take a comfortable chair near him. "Would you like something to drink?"

"No, thank you." Raven sat. "I came to warn you that Demetri is in town. I saw him at the club. Or at least I thought I did. When I went to check on it, to confirm it was him, he wasn't there."

"Yes. Demetri has arrived." Dafyd hoped he appeared calm, and not as if he was mentally picking out which room to lock her in. "He called here earlier this evening. He is planning on stopping by for a friendly chat at about eleven-thirty."

"Perhaps you're right, perhaps he doesn't know anything about me." The look on Raven's face led Dafyd to believe she was thinking furiously, and not really paying attention to what was going on around her.

"I have been considering options, since we last spoke." Dafyd stood. "I think it would be best to assume that he is here for two reasons. One to find you, since he is clearly obsessed with you. The second would be to eliminate me and take over here in LA." He walked to the door, motioning for her to follow. "Kill two birds with one stone as it were. It would make the most sense. You were right to come here. We should team up against him. If I may show you."

He took her to the room they had dubbed "the uninvited guests' room." It was a smallish room with a daybed disguised as a couch, a television set, a selection of games, and a few shelves of books. The only way in or out was through the door, a solid, sturdy, real wood door, with several locks on it.

Dafyd motioned to the window. The window was small circular, and didn't open. Raven peered out as Dafyd said, "If you look outside, you'll see that this house is well-guarded, with both a computerized security system, and old-fashioned vampire guards. The only people who get in are those we let in."

Raven looked around her at the room. She glanced back to the doorway, where Dafyd's bodyguard stood. "And the only ones who get out are those you let out."

"I apologize," Dafyd said. "But I cannot allow Demetri Vasile to get his hands on the crimson heir. I don't think anyone is ready for that new world order."

"I thought you didn't believe in that." Raven glared at him.

Spreading his hands, Dafyd said, "Demetri does. Others do. Perhaps in time I will also. But in the meantime, you must stay here. Demetri will not suspect you are here, and perhaps may never leave this building himself. I'm sorry. I can't risk you or my organization. I hope in time you will understand, and forgive me."

"I understand. But don't ever expect forgiveness."

CHAPTER EIGHTEEN

Jim watched in helpless horror as the vampire sank his fangs into Matt's neck, and Matt howled in agony, thrashing and writhing.

"No!" Vic screamed.

They all rushed forward, but the vampire hung onto Matt's now limp body, using it as a shield. He backed across the darkened sidewalk; the club's sign made Matt's face look strangely blue. The vampire hunters followed him, jockeying for the forward position in the crowd instead of fanning out into a circle in their usual attack formation.

Pulling a sharpened stake from his thigh pocket, Jim lifted it high preparing to plunge it into Matt's heart. It was the only thing Jim could do for him now.

"No!" Vic screamed a second time.

Jim felt someone grab his arm and pull back with all their might, flinging him backward. A couple of the guys stumbled around and over him. He lay stunned on the sidewalk, staring up at Vic.

"What were you doing?" Vic looked crazy.

"We've got to help Matt," Jim said.

"Yeah. Yeah." Vic helped Jim up. "We've got to get Matt." Vic looked around desperately.

Jim started forward again, only to see the vampire finish pulling Matt into a dark van and close the door.

"Stop that van!" Jim shouted, rushing towards the front of the van.

The other vampire hunters pounded on the side of the van, trying vainly to get the door open.

As the van started moving, Jim grabbed onto the windshield wiper and the side mirror, as if he could stop it. He managed to jump away safely before the van pulled away. Suddenly Vic's van was beside him.

"Get in." Vic was behind the wheel, staring at the retreating dark van. "Quick." He'd got the van moving before everyone was all the way in, but they did manage it, and no one was hurt.

The van careened through the night streets of LA in hot pursuit of the dark van. Light and darkness flashed through the interior of the van as they passed under streetlights and through darkened areas.

"Where's he going?" Truck asked.

"Don't know." Vic didn't take his eyes off the dark van.

"I know a short cut to the Embassy Suites," Mike said.

"We can't lose Matt," Vic said.

"Damn that bastard!" Jim found he had to wipe a tear from his eye. He couldn't remember ever being this scared or this helpless. Not since Tracey. One of their own, bitten by a vampire. Their greatest fear. Their worst nightmare come true.

Vic turned the corner sharply, and Jim found himself flung against the door with several others pushing him more forcefully into the door handle. Then suddenly they were released, and all righted themselves. Mike, Jim, Ekson, and Pete grabbed seat belts and secured themselves better. Truck riding shotgun did the same.

"Don't lose him," Mike said, his voice a low growl.

"Not a chance." The way Vic was sitting it looked almost like he wanted to crawl through the windshield. "I'm not about to let them do that to Matt."

"Where are they going?" Stevo asked.

"I don't know," Vic said.

"They don't seem to be trying to lose us," Truck said. "Odd."

"Think they're leading us into a trap?" Stevo said.

"I don't care," Vic said, "They can't have Matt."

Everyone fell silent after that, except for the occasional, "Watch out, they're turning," or "That left."

It felt to Jim that they had been tailing the van long enough to have reached Oregon by now, but the van's clock showed it had only been twenty minutes.

"I think I know where they're going!" Stevo said.

"I think you're right," Vic said. "We've got them now."

"Where?" Mike asked.

"The mansion we booby trapped today," Vic said.

"Couldn't be," said Pete.

Vic nodded. "Oh yeah. That's where they're going."

"I thought this Demetri wasn't from here," Jim said.

"Well you must have heard wrong," Truck said.

Mike leaned forward. "I was there too, I know what we heard. They don't know, or at least, don't like this Demetri."

"Doesn't matter. I'm going to let them think they've lost us." Vic kept going straight when the other van turned. "I know this neighborhood. We'll swing around the block here, and if I'm right we'll see them just parking in front of our target house. If not, we'll pick them up and keep following."

Jim realized he was breathing hard, and tried to relax. They swung around the block, and cruising slowly through one intersection, they all looked to see the dark van parked in front of the house.

"Turn," Jim said.

"No." Vic kept the van going straight, turning onto another block. "We're going to park in the alley a little ways behind the house. Then we'll figure out some way to get Matt back."

"Forget that," Mike said. "We've got to kill them all, Matt included. That's what we all swore."

Vic slowed the van to a stop. "We need Matt. We need his ideas and inventions. Could any of you have come up with the," Vic paused, waving his hands in frustration, before finally saying, "holy laser light?" Vic drew breath and shook his head. "Matt never even got to name his invention." He looked around at the rest of them. "Could any of you have done what he did? Could any of you have come up with a plan to booby trap a whole house to kill all the vampires inside?"

"No, but if he's a vampire, we've got to kill him," Mike said slowly. "We all swore."

"If." Vic nearly pounced on the word. "If. We don't even know if he is a vampire. Not all bites turn you. There are people who've been feeders for years."

"Yeah. 'Course nobody wants them hanging around forever," Truck muttered.

"Look, we'll find Matt. We'll rescue Matt." Vic nodded at the house. "Then we'll kill every monster inside."

There was a general murmur of agreement.

"Okay." Vic was back in his in charge mode now. "Truck, Stevo, Pete, go around the house, through the neighbor's yard. Check the van. If you find Matt, bring him back here. The rest of us will sneak in the back, kill any vampires we run into, and if Matt is in the house, we'll rescue him, then set the trap. Understood?"

"I think we need a bit more detail in our plan than just 'rescue Matt,'" Ekson said.

"Do you know where Matt is?" asked Vic. "Do you know if he's still unconscious? Do you know if they're locking him in a room, or just tormenting him by threatening to turn him, or just roughing him up?"

"No." Ekson shook his head.

"Okay, so we'll have to make it up as we go along," Vic growled. "Sorry. Ready?"

Everyone nodded.

"Let's go."

Truck, Stevo, and Pete headed off through the neighbor's yard. Vic, Ekson, Mike, and Jim headed for the house.

A vampire stood guard at the back gate. He didn't stand a chance against the massed frantic fury of the four vampire hunters. They left only one stake in his heart, Vic's, pulling the other three out.

"Bit of overkill there," Ekson said.

"No such thing with vampires," Mike said.

Adrenaline got them across the lawn, and up onto the porch. The back door was locked.

"Now what?" Mike asked. "It's too strong to break down."

"Back to the van." Vic said. "I've got tools there we can use to open the door."

Truck, Stevo, and Pete met them on the way back to the van.

"Weren't you going to get Matt from the van?" Vic asked.

Stevo shrugged. "He's not there. We saw the vampire that bit him escort him into the house."

"Okay." Vic paced as he thought. "We need to know where he's at. What they're doing to him."

"Can't we use the security system to find him?" Mike asked.

Vic stopped pacing and glared at Mike. "Yes, if we could get to the security room."

"It's right there," Mike said. "We were all in it today."

"That's just the utility room." Vic shook his head scornfully. "They wouldn't have even considered letting us change anything in their computer room."

"Oh."

"If we used just one or two people we could probably slip by them." Jim swum through the air making the motion of a fish tail. "After all, they do have company. We could just pretend to be one of Demetri's people. They'd only recognize us if we all stayed together."

Vic looked up triumphantly. "Yes. Who wasn't there

today? Who didn't work at the house? They'd have the best chance of getting through unnoticed."

"Ken and Woo had to work at their regular jobs today," Ekson said. "And no one has seen Lewis since last night."

Frowning, Vic looked around and asked, "Anybody know what happened to Lewis?"

They looked from one to another, but no one seemed to know.

"He musta left," Truck said. "He didn't seem to keen on attacking a whole houseful of vampires."

"Ken and Woo, too?" Vic asked.

A generalized shrug made its way through the group.

"They might have gotten stuck at work," Ekson said.

No one dared call the three missing men cowards. Even the ones that hadn't left were afraid. They didn't any of them want to do this, but they all felt they had to do something.

For themselves. For their loved ones. For Matt.

"So, everyone was at the house today?" Vic said with a sigh. "All right. Fine. Truck, you and I, we'll get Matt. The rest of you will guard our retreat, prepare the trap, and kill any vampires that try to stop you."

Everyone nodded.

"Let's get the tools and get back there," Vic said.

Truck reached in the van and grabbed a toolbox.

The small determined group of vampire hunters marched purposefully toward the back door.

CRIMSON HEIR

CHAPTER NINETEEN

Raven watched Dafyd pull the door closed, heard the click of locks on the other side of the door. Her calm veneer broke and she grabbed the closest object, the twenty-inch flat screen television, and hurled it. It smashed against the door with a crash of splintering glass and twisted plastic. The scrap bounced back, spreading debris from the door to halfway into the room. The door showed a scar, but not a big one.

Leaping forward, TV pieces crunching under her feet, Raven banged her fists against the door. "Let me out, I want out," she shouted.

Raven pounded a few more times, and then stopped. She realized that pounding and asking to be let out wasn't going to work. Dafyd had either been lying the entire time since she met him, Demetri had made an offer he couldn't refuse, or the lure of the prophecy had gotten to him. Either way he would pay.

Raven lived by the credo of never getting mad, don't stop with getting even, but get ahead. First she had to get out of the room, get someplace safe, and then work out a plan. Raven wouldn't let anyone control her, and Dafyd would pay for trying.

Moving through the room Raven searched for anything that would allow her to smash open the door, break the locks, something. She would try and pick the locks if she could find a paperclip. The fact that she had never picked a lock before was not going to stop her from trying.

Raven first checked the daybed couch. Her hope was that something had slipped out of a loose pocket and under the pillows and cushions at the back of the daybed. She tossed pillows and cushions aside, looked at the back where the mattress didn't quite meet the back, looked under it, and then threw the pieces back on in a pile. Nothing there.

She moved to the bookshelf next. The books were added to the couch pile. She ran her hand across the top of the bookcase and pulled back fingers coated with a thin layer of dust. When Raven pulled the two loose shelves from the case she looked at the window. She could easily break the glass with the boards, but the opening was too small for her to crawl through.

Besides, she told herself, the guards outside would be alerted and waiting for her. A lot of effort would only land her locked in another room. Or worse, in Demetri's control.

The thought of Demetri, coupled with the fact that he was going to be there soon, pushed Raven back into action. A quick check behind the bookcase revealed nothing of use. She didn't think any of the board games would provide her a hefty crowbar or 9mm, but she went through them.

There were no tools in the room that she could use. Leaning against the wall directly opposite of the door, Raven stared at it, trying to will it open. She was going to have to wait until someone came through. When that happened she wanted to be ready. She went to the pile on the couch and started to re-evaluate the contents for the purpose of mounting a defense or an attack.

Raven stopped, and looked back at the door. Maybe Dafyd had never used this room for holding a captive before, or maybe other captives hadn't noticed it. Raven couldn't believe her luck and went over to the door for a closer look. The hinges were on the inside.

There was nothing special about the pins, and Raven cast around the room looking for something she could use to push them out of place. There were no screwdrivers, but if she could find something with a flat edge she could use, then she could work on getting out.

Nothing on the bed was of use. Raven quickly discarded all of those items. She tried the edge of the shelf, but the wood splintered against the hinge. As she stood working the board against the hinge, Raven kept shifting her weight as she tried to get a purchase on the lip of the hinge pin with the board. The broken television pieces snapped and crunched under her feet.

Raven set the board down and picked up the television, the innards dangling in a long strand held together by wires and circuit boards. She saw a circuit board that might be of use and dropped the television again to try and break it out. It took a few tugs and twists, but she was able to break off the piece she needed.

Setting the metal against the hinge pin, Raven used the edge of the shelf to hammer lightly at the back of the circuit board. She tapped, trying to both be quiet and move the pin without forcing the circuit board to slip out of position. At first nothing seemed to be happening, but as Raven continued to apply light taps she saw the pin begin to move.

Hope came unbidden back into Raven's mind. She repositioned the circuit board into a better position that allowed her to hit with more effect. It only took her a few minutes to have the pins out of the hinges.

Raven pulled against the hinges and popped the door out after a few tries. The locks worked to hold the door in place, but Raven was able to pry the back of the door open wide enough to slip out. She took a moment to pull the door back into place as best she could.

Raven was now in the hallway, but had become disoriented. She was about half-way down a hall, and there were openings on either end, as well as doorways and openings on each side. She wished her excited state had allowed her to notice which direction she came, and which side the room door had been on. All of her worry about Demetri had worked against her.

Raven started down the hall to the left. She didn't hear anything, and hoped she could find a way to a back door. Mansions always had more than one door, and, if she could find one other than the front, she was going to slip out. Since guards routinely watch for people trying to break into a house, she hoped they wouldn't be looking for someone trying to break out.

When she reached the end of the corridor, Raven paused and slowly looked around the edge of the wall. She pulled back fast, hoping she hadn't been seen. Demetri was there. He had been in a room across the grand two-story foyer, near the staircase she'd come up. This time she was sure it was him. He was looking at someone else, but Raven was afraid he'd seen her.

Moving more for speed and less for stealth, Raven ran back down the hallway the other direction. At the intersection she paused and again peered around the corner. No one. A staircase led both down and up. Raven tiptoed down to another hallway.

This one looked like it led to the back of the house. Raven moved along the hall, her back pressed against one wall, her head pivoting back and forth, trying to watch where she was going and where she had been both at the same time.

Raven passed a couple of closed doors. She didn't know where they led, or who might be behind them, so she continued past. She reached a large open door by the end of the hallway. Raven slowed to look around the corner into the room. She allowed herself to take a deep breath when she saw a large, shadowy, open room with a door to the outside.

There was no one in the room and Raven stepped in. The door had a glass window in the upper half and Dafyd had heavy black curtains installed over it, but Raven was able to push the curtain aside enough to peek out.

She looked out into the dark grounds of the mansion and was about to step out and make a run for the back wall when she detected movement in the yard. She watched and saw several people headed for the door. Too many to fight quietly, so she pulled back.

She didn't want to get caught, so she moved toward the main hallway. If she could get to one of those other doors, she could hide inside. Raven was desperate and ready to kill anyone that might stop her from hiding and escaping.

When she was about to step back into the hallway, Raven heard soft voices headed her way. Someone was coming from that direction too.

Turning back into the room, Raven searched for somewhere to hide. The room was a mud room, with furniture consisting of hooks, shelves, and a sink. There was nothing big enough to hide behind or under.

Raven spotted a door, about two-thirds the height of a regular door, tucked back in a corner. She rushed over to it and slowly twisted the doorknob and pulled it open, hoping it would be silent. Inside Raven found a vacuum cleaner, brooms, mops, and shelves of cleaning supplies against the far wall. It was a tight squeeze, but Raven didn't have any choice. She forced herself into the broom closet, sitting on top of the vacuum, and closed the door just as the voices from the corridor entered the room.

CHAPTER TWENTY

Dafyd stood as Marlynne ushered Demetri Vasile in. Dafyd's four bodyguards remained where they were, one seated behind and to the left of Dafyd, one standing at the window, one standing in the corner, and one standing to the left of the door.

Four men accompanied Demetri, which squared with the information Dafyd had obtained earlier. Though Dafyd was surprised to see that they went everywhere with Demetri; Dafyd would have left one or two to guard their hotel rooms or their rented vehicle. However, not everyone was the same. Demetri's clothes bore this out. Dafyd had expected Demetri to prefer suits— business attire, yet here Demetri was in a leather jacket and black jeans.

Though perhaps it was a ruse intended to give credence to Demetri's "vacation."

Time to play the game. Dafyd shrugged it off, smiled at Demetri and extended his hand toward his nemesis.

"Welcome. You must be Demetri Vasile. I'm Dafyd Peack." After a brief, firm handshake, he motioned to the other men. "And these gentlemen?"

"My associates." Demetri waved his hand at each man as he spoke their names. "Finian Jordan, Burt Osborn, Trigg Robinson, and Matthew Mann."

Like Demetri, the first three men were medium tall, strongly built, and tough looking. Their faces were set as if in masks of bored blankness. The last one, however, was short, slender, and geeky looking. His expression bore a striking resemblance to a rabid squirrel—wide eyes that looked as if they'd never seen the world before. His gaze darted around in stunned surprise at chairs, carpet, curtains, people, everything. His mouth kept opening and closing, but he made no noise. His hands shook nervously.

"Please, be seated. Make yourselves comfortable." Dafyd crooked his finger at Marlynne standing in the doorway. "May I offer you some refreshment? We have fresh blood and aged blood for those that like it. Or water." After listening to their requests, Dafyd turned to Marlynne, "Nine fresh bloods and a tray, please."

The strange little Matthew had timidly refused any drink. Demetri chose a seat near Dafyd, and as he relaxed back into the cushions, his three bodyguards selected spots throughout the room. Matthew however, began pacing near the door.

Seating himself back in his chair, Dafyd smiled at Demetri. "Enjoying your vacation so far?"

"We've only just arrived," Demetri said.

Ah, the wealth of meaning in that statement. Dafyd

kept smiling. "I understand, but there's so much to do in LA. You wouldn't want to miss anything."

Demetri smiled tightly. "Speaking of missing something. One of my people is missing. I was wondering if perhaps you've seen her."

"Missing someone already?" Dafyd allowed his real amusement at the verbal sparing to come through. "Since you've only just arrived, I'd suspect someone has gone off for a little 'r 'n r' on their own."

"She actually arrived a couple of weeks ago on her vacation. Her name is Lucrecia Lute. She never returned home." Demetri's blank face was back.

Matthew started breathing hard, and wringing his hands.

Pretending not to notice Matthew, Dafyd said, "Oh, I see. Well, I wish I could help you. I've never met her." Dafyd shrugged. "LA has so many vampires, some permanent residents, some just passing through. I can't keep track of all of them."

"Still, we will be looking for her. Along with taking care of our other business." Demetri paused as Marlynne returned with two others vampires, all bearing trays.

Marlynne passed out the drinks, to Demetri first, then his men, then Dafyd's guards, and lastly, Dafyd. The two vampires with her placed small plates containing various nibblets on the low tables near each of them.

One of the two with Marlynne, a younger looking female vampire, smiled at Matthew, and said, "Canapé, sir?"

"What?" Matthew looked at her in wild-eyed surprise, and came to a full stop.

"Well, we have black pudding." She pointed to a couple of pieces on the last remaining plate on her tray. "Then there's caviar in blood aspic, marrow medallions, and fried arteries."

Matthew stared at her in open-mouthed surprise.

After a moment her smile slipped. "I'll just set it here, shall I?" She placed the plate onto the corner of a desk near where Matthew had been pacing. His gaze followed the plate, and remained anchored there after the young woman scurried out.

Watching this Dafyd couldn't help asking, "Is he all right?"

"He's just a bit," Demetri paused, "new to our ways. Perhaps it would be best if he took some air." The last sentence seemed to be directed toward Matthew.

Turning from the canapés, Matthew blinked at Demetri several times. "Yes. Yes, that is a good idea." Matthew looked over to Dafyd. "May I go out? To your backyard."

"Marlynne," Dafyd said, "would you be so kind as to escort our young guest outside."

"Of course." Marlynne put one hand gently on Matthew's elbow. "If you will just come with me."

She and Matthew followed after her assistants, and she shut the door.

Dafyd raised his glass, gently swirling the blood. "To the game that is life." Nodding slightly to his guests, he added, "Even if you're undead."

The rest of the room raised their glasses to the toast, then sipped.

Demetri raised his glass. "To old friends, and new."

Not a chance, Dafyd thought as he sipped. Not if he

could help it. Thinking about Raven, safely stashed in the room down the hall, Dafyd knew this game would go to him.

"So," Demetri said as he picked up a marrow medallion on a stick, "Other than the Disney parades, is there any other nightlife in LA we shouldn't miss?"

Pushing a different pawn out, thought Dafyd. For a moment Dafyd didn't know whether to be relieved or annoyed that Demetri was dropping the subject of Lucrecia. It was a relief not to have to continue pretending he didn't know anything, but annoying in that Dafyd had hoped to provoke Demetri into giving Dafyd's guards an excuse to eliminate Demetri. Dafyd managed a tight smile. "I know that New York has a reputation as the city that never closes, but I'm of the opinion that LA's nightlife is much better."

"Oh?" Demetri's exclamation didn't even bother to be provocative or inquiring.

"Yes." Dafyd picked up a piece of black pudding from the plate near his elbow. "Of course, it all depends on your tastes. There are shows, restaurants, clubs, the beach. Many tourists like to watch movies being filmed. They do that even at night." At Demetri's raised eyebrows, Dafyd added, "I find that rather boring. They waste too much time, and I don't see the point in repeating the entire thing for one tiny change."

"Something we agree upon." Demetri sipped his blood. "Actually I have an interest in the club scene. I'm always looking for new talent."

"I didn't think you were just here for a fun jaunt." Dafyd tipped his glass to Demetri and sipped. "Business and pleasure, eh?"

So far all of Demetri's guards had kept their blank faces up. Though Dafyd suspected that the one by the window had a particular liking for marrow medallions, as no more remained on his plate while the rest sat.

"As you say." Demetri turned over a fried artery on his plate as if considering it. "I've heard good things about a group called the Sinister Sisters."

"Yes, I have heard them mentioned. By the younger vampires, the Goths I believe." Dafyd turned to the guard sitting behind him. "Have you heard of them?"

"Yes, sir." Felton nodded. "They've been playing down at the Club. Goth band, very good."

"Which club?" Dafyd asked, as if he didn't already know.

"The Club, sir," Felton said. "It's a Goth club, named The Club. I've a flyer downstairs."

"I see. Thank you, that won't be necessary." Dafyd turned back to Demetri, and smiled. "There you have it."

"You're not much into the Goth scene?" Demetri said.

"No. Nor you, I suspect. My background is more," Dafyd held up a piece of black pudding on a stick, "Celtic."

Demetri waved all this away. "More to the business end, I understand that not only are they good music wise, but they are very good-looking. And the lead singer is supposed to be a vampire, Khalida Raven."

"As I've said, I don't know every vampire in town." Dafyd raised his eyebrows at Demetri. "If I spent all my time meeting vampires I'd never get any business done."

Pursing his lips as if having tasted something sour, Demetri picked up his glass, then drained the contents. "Good cellar you have."

"Thank you."

"But as you say, if I spend all my time talking I won't get any business done."

Dafyd nodded. "So, how long will you be in town?"

"Long enough to conduct my business, and have a little fun." Demetri stood, and so did his guards.

Slowly getting to his feet, as if reluctant to end the interview, Dafyd motioned to his guards to do the same. "Let me know if there is anything I, or my people, can assist you with." The only help Dafyd intended to give Demetri was to get him from undead to completely dead.

"Very kind." Demetri headed for the door. "I will let you know."

Dafyd hurried to put himself next to Demetri, rather than let any of the guards get between them. He wanted to do the honors to Demetri himself. Behind him, guards jockeyed for position. Dafyd knew his guards were picking out which of Demetri's guards they were going to kill. Dafyd wondered what excuse the extra guard would use to get to Matthew to do him in.

At the bottom of the stairs, Demetri seemed to remember his errant associate. "We'll need to collect Matthew."

Signaling to the extra guard, Dafyd said, "Find Marlynne and young Matthew."

"They went out back," Marlynne's youthful female assistant said, motioning back down the hall. She slipped by, presumably to go clean up in the blue parlor.

The guard walked down the hall, and opened the door to another hallway.

Dafyd was watching Demetri watch the guard. Suddenly Demetri's eyes went wide, and he whispered, "Khalida."

Demetri shoved past Dafyd, down the hall after the guard. With fury at so rude a treatment as his excuse, and eager to kill Demetri, Dafyd started after him.

CHAPTER TWENTY-ONE

Jim brought up the rear of the group as they headed determinedly toward the back door. He looked around the dark for anyone from the house, but saw no one.

The only light in the backyard came from the lights in the windows of the house. The corner streetlights were too far away to cast any light in the backyard. Luckily the house's owner preferred a smooth lawn with only a few trees, rather than the current vogue for water features, statuary, raised garden beds, and any number of seats or benches.

Huddled by the door on the porch in the dark, Vic and Truck fumbled with the tools. Jim started to worry about how much time they were taking and how much noise might be heard. His own heartbeat could surely be heard throughout the neighborhood.

Suddenly Vic and Truck backed away from the door, nearly knocking everyone behind them down. The sound of voices and the turning of the knob startled everyone. There was a mad rush for the walls.

It opened and two silhouetted figures appeared in the doorway. Both stepped out, and the door closed. Before any of the vampire hunters could react, one vampire tackled the other. Both fell toward the stairs.

The vampire hunters piled on, pinning both figures to the ground. Jim felt someone grab his ankle, and he slid off the pile. He held onto his stake, looking for somewhere in the shadowy pile to thrust it in. In the dark all the figures looked alike.

The light spilling from the open door occasionally revealed one face or another, but by the time Jim realized who it was he couldn't see them anymore. Amazingly there was no screaming and very little noise from the pile-up.

Ekson looked up, horrified. His face was replaced by a woman's, but Jim could see only a portion of her face. Vic's face and Stevo's rolled by fast. The whole pile was edging slowly toward the stairs.

Temporarily abandoning the stake, Jim grabbed the nearest arm, trying to either pull someone out or halt the inexorable slide to the stairs. Instead he was pulled with them, managing to stop himself on his knees at the top step. The man whose arm he'd grabbed lay sprawled across the steps moaning from the bruising of several bodies sliding down him and crushing him.

The sprawling mass of people at the bottom of the stairs began sorting themselves out. Jim watched as Mike suddenly realized that the person he was climbing off of was a woman. Mike's stake was out, and he'd run her through, before she could react.

Truck helped Vic and Pete to their feet. Everyone was

looking around to figure out who was who, whispering names and checking faces. Jim reached down to grab the hair on the head now moaning at the stairs. He lifted the head so that he could see the face.

"Matt!" Jim whispered.

"Where?" asked Vic, rushing over.

"There." Jim dropped his hold on Matt's hair and arm, and turned to find his abandoned stake.

"Matt!" Vic rushed over to turn Matt over. "Get him up."

Truck lifted Matt just as Jim found his stake. He hurried over, but Vic wouldn't let him stake Matt. Vic put himself between Jim and Matt. "No, we need him."

"Are you crazy? He's a vampire now," Jim said.

"At least let me check. Let's go inside into the light and check," Vic whispered urgently. "Then we can set off the trap. Come on."

Vic pushed Jim into the house, followed closely by Mike, Pete, and Ekson. Truck and Stevo carried Matt into the house, then past everyone else into the utility room just off the mud room. Mike turned the light on.

The booby trap controls waited for them on the wall by the window, but everyone ignored them. Truck and Stevo propped Matt up against the wall, both supporting him and trapping him there. Vic carefully pulled back Matt's upper lip.

"See he's not a vampire," Vic said without looking.

The rest of the vampire hunters gasped.

"He's got fangs," Ekson said.

Vic turned to look. Matt's eyes slowly opened and focused on Vic.

"Get your hand away from his mouth!" Jim said.

"Quiet!" Vic whispered as he pulled his hand away.

"He's a vampire we've got to kill him." Jim held up his stake. "I'll do it."

"No! We need him," Vic said.

"Yeah, Vic. I'm a vampire now," Matt said. "Kill me before I bite you,"

"No. We can help him. Yes, yes," Vic said. "We'll figure out a way. A way to cure vampires. Yes. Matt's smart enough to do that."

"Matt doesn't want to," Matt said. "Matt likes being a vampire, look what he can do." With a sudden burst of strength Matt threw Truck and Stevo off of him, but before he could recover his balance, Truck, Stevo, Pete, and Ekson had all piled onto him, slamming him down onto the floor. Pinning him where he couldn't bite them.

"We have to stake him now, and set the booby trap off," Jim said. "They're going to discover us soon. Let me through."

"Not now." Matt squirmed under his captors. "Demetri needs to get out first."

Vic kept himself between Jim and Matt. "No. We need him. We need his ideas. We can contain him until we can cure him."

"There is no cure. Matt wouldn't want to be a vampire." Jim strained to push past Vic.

"Poor Jim," said Matt, "Poor, sweet, innocent Jim The only honest man among us." Matt laughed. "He was the only one that meant it when he swore to stake us if we ever turned vampire, and the only one we could really trust to do it. He hunts vampires for his sister, you know. Certain that no one would ever want to continue as a vampire." Matt looked at Jim. "What did your sister say when you staked her? Did she beg you to kill her, or beg you to leave her alone? She didn't want you to do it, you know. I don't want you to do it. And never fear, Vic won't let you." The look in Matt's eyes was feral. "Vic does it for the power. Truck and Stevo for the sheer love of killing. But noble, stupid Jim only does it because he truly believes that it's the right thing to do." Matt laughed. "No, don't stake me. I want this. This power, this control. You have no idea how it feels. Finally I have everything I ever wanted. You think you have me? You think you can stake me? Watch this."

With a might heave, Matt threw all four men off him and jumped up. He stood between them and the control box. "It won't work. I didn't set it right this afternoon. I didn't want anyone to accidentally set it off. So until I wire it properly, it won't work. In the meantime, I think I could use a light snack." He lunged at Vic, mouth open, poised to bite, and collapsed.

Mike grinned and held up his taser. "Electricity always works."

"So what about the booby trap?" Stevo asked.

"It's got to work," Ekson said. "He knew what he was doing this afternoon. He didn't mention anything about not setting it up correctly then. He has to be lying, because he's a vampire."

Jim opened his mouth, but couldn't bring himself to say anything. He couldn't quit thinking about what Matt had said.

Did they all think he was stupid and foolish?

Sometimes Jim thought himself stupid. He remembered all the times he'd truly felt like the ignorant hick he so often acted like. It had been such an easy act. Or had he not been acting, but just being himself.

Around him the other vampire hunters argued, but he didn't care. Jim just held his stake loosely in his hand, and stared at Matt's limp body.

Matt had said he didn't want to be staked. Was that real? The old Matt had sworn he wanted to be staked if he were turned. Yet, now, he claimed he didn't.

Had Tracey truly meant it when she begged Jim not to do it? He hadn't believed her. Hadn't wanted to believe she really liked being a vampire. Jim had believed she was only hurting herself and everyone around her. Tracey wouldn't want that, would she? No, Tracey had never wanted to hurt anyone.

But what if she'd meant it when she'd promised she'd never bite anyone that didn't want her to, that she wouldn't hurt anyone. As she begged, she to had said that it felt wonderful being a vampire.

Jim closed his eyes. In his memory he saw the life drain out of Tracey's eyes. How could she really be undead, soulless, if there was still life in those eyes?

"I say we set off the trap. If it doesn't work then we can either fix it or stake every vampire in the place," said Truck.

"Yes, yes. You're right," Vic said. "But let me get Matt out of here. Then you can let loose the holy laser light."

"I don't think you'll be doing that," said a voice from the doorway.

Jim opened his eyes and turned around with the rest of the vampire hunters.

A lanky, dark-haired vampire in a western outfit and boots stood in the doorway.

CHAPTER TWENTY-TWO

Raven huddled in the closet near the door. She wanted to be able to leave quickly, as soon as the opportunity presented itself. Worse case, if she was discovered she wanted to be in a position to leap out and attack whoever opened the door. If they weren't sure she was inside, a fast attack followed by an even faster sprint into the night might get her free.

The cleaning products lining the shelf against the back wall weren't closed very well. Pine scent battled bleach to see which could make Raven's eyes water the most. Raven opened her mouth, afraid that she would sneeze or worse. Using the sleeve of her shirt, Raven wiped her eyes and her nose. She pressed her ear to the door.

Whoever it was that she had heard coming to the mud room from inside the house had gone outside. Raven decided to give them a few minutes before attempting to sneak out. If they were going to meet the others she saw in the yard, they might be coming back in. Raven wanted to get out of that house so bad, and then just keep going. Her short time locked in that room had convinced her that there was no way she was going to let anyone keep her locked up and under their control.

When no one returned from the outside after a couple of minutes Raven decided to check things out. She eased the door open and began to shift her weight to leave her confined hiding place, but a commotion outside the back door made her stop.

The noise sounded like a fight was going on, and it was heading for the door. Raven ducked back into the closet, pulling the door partly closed before several men shoved their way into the room. She held the door still and hoped no one noticed it was ajar. Raven looked through the sliver of a view at what was happening in the room.

Raven watched as several men struggled with one man, forcing him into another room across the mud room from where she hid. As she listened she got the gist of the problem. These were friends of someone who was now a vampire. The vampire wanted to be a vampire, but the norms were upset about it. It wasn't like being a vampire was a cult, and they could unbrainwash someone back into old behavior, attitudes, and living in the sunlight.

Listening further, Raven realized she was wrong. These were vampire hunters and they had some sort of nasty plan for Dafyd and his followers. A doomsday device of some sort had been installed in the house and every vampire there was going to die if they didn't get out. She would die if she didn't get out.

Raven looked through the opening again, but couldn't see anyone in the other room. She started to slip out of hiding, hoping to make it to the door before the vampire hunters noticed her, but as she stuck her head out she saw the back door opening slowly. Raven ducked back into hiding, wanting to run so bad her leg muscles were twitching.

When she looked again, Raven saw the back of a tall man in the doorway to the room where the vampire hunters had their booby trap. The crack was too small to let her see much detail, and Raven was afraid of who it might be. A tall male all dressed in black, exactly like Demetri had looked at the club. She couldn't help but worry that he had seen her upstairs, and was now searching for her. Her flight reflex was kicking in.

Raven was preparing to jump out, shove the person across from her into the other room with the vampire hunters, and make a run for it in the confusion. Then she heard him speak.

"I don't think you'll be doing that," said Cowboy.

Cowboy! Raven let hope creep back in and she allowed herself to believe she would be able to escape. Raven eased the door open and slipped out of hiding.

"And who are you to stop us? There's one of you and eight of us," said a voice from inside the room.

"Eight of you against one vampire is true, but we're in close quarters here. Which of you is ready to join my side tonight," said Cowboy.

"Come on guys, let's get him, there's only one of 'em," said the voice in the room.

"Two," said Raven as she stepped up next to Cowboy.

Raven gazed up at Cowboy and was gratified to see the look of surprise in his eyes. It wasn't often she surprised him.

"Two," Cowboy said, turning back to look at the norms in the room.

Eight norms stood in the room in various stances of fighting readiness. One lay on the floor. Based on what she had heard, Raven took to be their recently transformed friend.

"Come on. Let's get them and get out of here," said the voice Raven had heard before.

She could see that the voice belonged to a disheveled man who gripped a wooden stake so hard that Raven could see his white knuckles. The looks of the others in the room told Raven that despite his bravado, this one was not the leader. The others looked to the one standing over the prone vampire.

Raven watched as Cowboy feinted a lunge at the gung-ho vampire hunter. Whatever it was he expected to happen was obviously not what did happen. While seven of the vampire hunters shrunk back away from Cowboy, the crazed one with the stake charged, dropping his stake and attacking with his bare hands.

As Cowboy retreated into her, trying to fend off the lunatic norm, he pushed Raven back. She tried to reach in and punch the norm from the side, but only landed a glancing blow. The push of bodies forced her off balance, and she and Cowboy had to fall even further back or be knocked over.

The other norms followed the lead of the first and surged out of the utility room at them. Raven and Cowboy tried to fight side by side to push back the onslaught of the vampire hunters. There wasn't enough room, and they kept getting in each others' way. Raven threw blows that would have broken bones or knocked the hunters unconscious, but her punches were deflected by Cowboy's similar attempts. The only consolation was the hunters were having an equally hard time striking them.

The surprise of the attack, followed up with the force of numbers, pushed Raven and Cowboy away from the back door and into the hallway of the house.

"No," said Raven as she saw the door to freedom get farther away from her. She planted her feet and refused to give another step. Her hands blurred as she landed blow after blow, deflecting a fist coming at her face with her forearms.

Three of the norms were attacking her and Cowboy at the same time. Cowboy was deflecting their blows toward him, aiming and timing his counter punches for maximum effect. Raven was too frantic, knowing that to lose here would doom her to death at the hands of these hunters, or worse, an eternity of being a captive of one of the power brokers in the other room.

The norm directly in front of Raven was standing with his left foot forward, right foot back, protecting his maleness from Raven's foot. Instead she kicked at his left knee, hoping to cripple him in a painful way that might slow the other hunters and allow the tide of the fight to change directions.

The norm must have seen it coming. He moved his knee at the last second, and Raven was pulled off balance. She twisted her torso, and the powerful punch aimed at her chest smashed against her left arm with numbing force. Raven recovered her footing, but she had to give a few feet of hallway to do it.

Cowboy stepped back, and again they blocked the hunters from working their way around them. Three hunters fought directly in front of them with the others trying to push forward and join in the fray. Raven and Cowboy again were holding them in check.

Raven heard the bellow of the largest norm in the group, stuck in the back of the pack. He surged forward, pushing against the backs of his friends, forcing them forward and into Raven and Cowboy. The hunters were pushed into them with such force they knocked both Raven and Cowboy back against the corridor walls.

Raven crashed into the wall, smashing her left shoulder as she hit the wall and spun away to avoid any follow up blows. Her left arm was feeling the pain of the fight. It throbbed when she moved it. It was harder for her to raise it to fight, but it was fight or die. She had lived for a long time and knew wounds could be treated after winning the battle. During battle there was only victory or death.

Cowboy had been pushed into the opposite wall and had stopped farther down from the door than Raven. They were now separated by about six feet of corridor. The three hunters they had been exchanging punches with had been knocked off balance as well. One was on the floor on his hands and knees, and the other two were recovering where they had hit the walls. The hunters that had been behind them surged forward.

Two managed to get behind Raven, and they attacked Cowboy while she fought two in front of her. She was grateful that the fight had been fast and chaotic. None of the hunters had tried using a stake. No bottles of holy water were thrown at them. Fists and feet were the weapons being used, and she and Cowboy responded in kind.

Raven felt pain shoot through her left arm as she blocked another punch. Her nostrils flared as she grunted from the force of the blow. Raven bared her fangs and hissed at her attackers. It seemed to surprise them as they slowed their attack for a second.

A second was what she needed. She spun half way around and grabbed one of the hunters fighting Cowboy by the back of his shirt and pulled him around away from Cowboy. He spun as she turned him, losing his balance and stumbling as Raven shoved him into the two hunters she had been fighting. She stepped back to stand next to Cowboy and helped him fight the hunter he was fending off, the large one that had pushed them deep down the corridor.

The other hunters joined in again. Raven and Cowboy were driven back further. Caught up in the exchange of blows, Raven didn't realize how much ground they were giving up until it was too late.

"Khalida," Raven heard from behind her. The voice was one she had prayed to never hear again. Demetri.

"We've got to get out of here," Raven said to Cowboy. They had backed up nearly to the foyer.

Cowboy punched one hunter, then spun and planted his elbow into the solar plexus of another. He looked Raven in the eye.

"Darlin', I've been working on that for a couple of

minutes now," said Cowboy, before turning back and blocking an oncoming double handed swing that had been aimed at the back of his head.

Raven tried to push forward, run through the hunters, force a wedge through them so she could escape. She felt solid punches land on her head and side. Other blows glanced off other parts of her body. The strikes were so intense she couldn't move forward and was forced back next to Cowboy.

Raven struck back, hitting one hunter twice in his chest before feeling her arm grabbed from behind.

"Khalida, I've been looking everywhere for you. Let me help you get out of here," said Demetri.

Demetri held Raven with a bone-crushing grip by her left forearm. The pain was so intense she cried out. It felt like hot fire being shoved through her arm and into her brain. Raven felt herself being pulled away from Cowboy.

"No," Raven shouted.

She spun and brought her fist around, hitting Demetri in the face. Demetri let go of her arm as his hands went to his face. Beyond Demetri, Raven could see Dafyd and several other vampires all converging on them.

"Kill them all, except for Khalida Raven," shouted Dafyd.

Feral screams filled the air as vampire attacked vampire. Hunter fought vampire, and Cowboy and Raven fought off attackers from both sides. Raven could see Cowboy was growing weary. He was favoring his right leg, and his punches didn't seem to be having the same impact as when the fight started. She moved to him, and together they were able to get their backs against a wall. Now they only had to fend off attacks from one side.

Raven saw Demetri try to come to her again. Dafyd attacked him from behind, pushing him to the ground. The two rolled on the floor, fangs bared, fists punching, fingers clawing at throats and eyes.

Raven fought back against one of Dafyd's serving girl vampires. It was obvious that she wasn't used to fighting and Raven was able to toss her at a group of other vampires, knocking the entire group off balance.

"Do you see any opening down the hallway?" Raven asked Cowboy as she kicked one of the vampire hunters in the stomach.

Cowboy turned to look. "No, that way is filled with fighting. Do you think we can get to the front door?"

Raven looked at Demetri and Dafyd rolling and scrambling along the floor as they continued to fight each other. Bodyguards for each fought around them while trying to help their perspective boss.

"Doesn't look good that way either," said Raven. "I'm not sure how we're going to get out of here."

CHAPTER TWENTY-THREE

The jumble spilled down the hall. Fists flew in every direction. A kicking, gouging, scratching ball of twisted bodies surged forward and back, following tidal forces of its own making. The sheer difficulty of recognizing friend and foe in the bewilderingly crowded swirl of faces, legs, backs, chests, arms, feet, and fists, kept everyone from using lethal force for the moment. The hallway's walls and doors absorbed, or broke under, the force of misplaced blows.

Screams and shouts mingled with moans, thumps, crashes, and ominous bone cracking sounds. The fight grew as people from other parts of the house found themselves sucked into the dizzying melee.

Trays, chairs, small tables, knick-knacks, wall sconces, ornamental shelves—whatever loose or semi-detached item that fell within the sphere of influence of the brawl became weapons in the ever-inventive hands of the participants. One wall broke under repeated blows, and a small knot of combatants surged through seeking space for their immediate quarrels.

Unfortunately, the space was merely a linen closet. Shelves, towels, and bed sheets exploded into the main fracas in the hallway, spreading more chaos and making the footing treacherous for all involved.

For a wild, terrifying moment no one dared stop for fear of being overcome and trampled. Screams reached an appalling pitch, and the blows became fiercer and more dangerous. The fight's fury reached the feral vicious brutality of a crazed mob high on adrenaline.

An odd buzzing spark sent one of the vampire hunters to the floor.

"Mike, it's too crowded," shouted Vic.

Something in the battle broke like a wave on the ocean tumbling over its crest to roar foaming down to the beach. The scuffle surged to the rear of the house, as the vampire hunters made an abrupt, unrehearsed, and, above all, swift retreat.

Vic stumbled through the utility room, with one eye swollen closed, to find Matt's still unconscious body. He grabbed Matt's wrists and began pulling him from the room. His exit was temporarily blocked by the fighting.

Mike waved his taser at anyone that got near him, trying to bring up the rear and protect the other vampire hunters. This maneuver trapped several vampires behind him, who frantically fought anyone near them as they dithered over breaking out of the entire skirmish with these strangers or fighting their way back to their own kind.

Stevo grabbed his stake firmly in his right hand, and

dragged Pete by his shirt with his left from the floor where Pete had fallen. By flailing the stake through the air he was able to cut a path through the fight.

Ekson kicked his way to the rear, cradling his broken right arm, sobbing.

Truck found Vic at the doorway to the utility room dragging Matt. He helped clear a path and carry Matt.

Ten people stumbled out into the dark on the back porch. For a moment it looked at if the entire fight might follow them.

"Get out of my way," a lanky vampire shouted as he pushed the next emerging vampire back into the house. "Raven!"

The other two vampires followed him inside, and the fight recoiled back the way it had come.

"Mike, help me. Pete got hit by your taser," Stevo said as he wrestled Pete down the stairs.

Mike and Stevo carried Pete. Vic and Truck carried Matt. Ekson limped along behind them.

"What happened to Jim?" Mike asked.

"Dunno." Truck spit a dark, glistening glob into the shadows. "I haven't seen him since all those vampires joined the fight."

They paused by the van, their unconscious comrades half in the open doors to look back at the house.

"We gotta go back for him," Mike said.

"If he's still in there, he's dead," Ekson said.

"Jim's nowhere near as helpless as everyone thinks." Vic began wrestling Matt into the van again. "He can get himself out of there if that's what he really wants."

"What about the booby trap?" Ekson asked.

"You want to go set it off?" Vic asked. Ekson shook his head no. Vic looked at the rest of them. "Anyone else want to volunteer?" No one did.

They all piled into the van, except Mike who kept looking back at the house. "Wait. I keep thinking Jim'll come running out of there. He's got to."

"Come on," Vic shouted at him as he started the van.

The back door of the house remained open, but no one emerged from the door.

Mike sighed, jumped into the van, and closed the door. The van rolled away in the night.

The brawl headed back into the well-lit hall, where the participants could see each other better, and where there was more room.

Raven stood silently just inside the utility room. Jim stood beside a control box by the window, his stake held loosely in his left hand. He hadn't moved for some time now.

"What is that?" she asked.

He blinked at her. "We rigged the whole house, fiber optics, holy water, and new lights. Matt said the lights wouldn't be as effective as lasers, but with enough of them they'd work."

"What do they do?" Raven didn't dare move toward him. She didn't know if he realized he had one hand on a switch at the control box or if he was awaiting some planned signal to set it off. He didn't look quite sane to her.

"Holy laser light," Jim whispered. "Should destroy all the vampires in the house without harming any ordinary people or the house itself."

Raven mind boggled with the possibilities. It couldn't work. Or could it? "Do you think it'll work?"

"It did on Lucrecia." Jim looked at her, stared at her with eyes that were bleak and hollow. "She turned inside out, into a skeleton, into a statue of blood. It was," he paused and swallowed hard, "horrible. There was nothing left. Not even ashes."

Searching frantically, Raven tried to think of the right words to get him to move away from the machine.

"Do you hurt people?" Jim asked.

Taken a bit by surprise at the turn in the conversation, Raven said, "Not intentionally. I will defend myself, of course, but I don't go out looking for trouble." Perhaps there was something she could say to get him away from the switch. "If you leave me alone, I'll leave you alone."

Obviously those weren't the right words. He seemed more confused and disturbed, rather than less. He asked, "Are you in pain? Does it hurt being you?"

"No more than it hurts being you," Raven said.

Jim smiled at her. He walked over to stand in front of her, his hand tightening on his stake. Raven held absolutely, perfectly still.

"If you see Tracey, tell her I'm sorry." He leaned over to kiss her on the cheek. "It's yours." Then he left.

Raven wasn't sure who Tracey was, but at the moment she didn't care. She heard the sound of the back door closing followed by footsteps across the porch and down the steps. Raven raced to the control panel, and opened it.

The insides made no sense to her. She didn't know if it would really do what Jim had said it would, but the thought of being able to rid herself of all those who'd tried to control her was very tempting. The merest flick of her finger, the tiniest motion, and they'd die.

Closing the box, Raven realized she'd have to find Cowboy. They had to get out of here. Then, maybe she could see if the trap really worked, or perhaps it would be best to just pull the guts out of it, before the vampire wars escalated to a whole new level.

Find Cowboy first.

Moving to the utility room's doorway, Raven cautiously peered out into the mud room. The mud room itself wasn't filled with the ongoing brawl, but occasionally someone would pop in, either by choice or tossed in, only to bounce back into the fray. The original purpose of the fight forgotten, the combatants having regressed into a primal state, fighting for the lust of blood, of revenge.

Carefully choosing her moment, Raven dashed out of the utility room and across the mud room to the opposite side of the hall doorway. The door itself had been wrenched from its frame and lay in two pieces on the floor.

As she passed by the doorway, Raven caught a glimpse of the fight. Demetri and Dafyd were locked in a clinch, each pounding the others ribs, but unable to get the upper hand in the treacherous footing in the hallway and random motion of the combatants.

Daring a second peek, Raven nearly had her head

taken off as a woman flew past into the mud room. Raven didn't recognize her. However, she wasn't a concern for Raven since she lay unconscious where she slumped against the sink.

Her third glimpse proved more productive. Cowboy was about halfway down the hall, through the fight, and appeared to be heading away from her.

Raven didn't dare jump into the fight. The chances of her becoming the wishbone in a tug of war between Dafyd and Demetri, and their people, were too great. A shout would get her too much attention, but she had no other way to contact him.

Someone's cell phone started ringing, and Raven wished again that she had one. She could've called Cowboy.

Taking a deep breath, Raven cupped her hands around her mouth and shouted, "Cowboy!"

Cowboy's head turned to look at her, as did Dafyd's and Demetri's. Cowboy started fighting his way back to her. Providentially, Cowboy shoved the grappling Dafyd and Demetri into a large dent in the wall, opening a new hole in the wall. Raven doubted that it was deliberate, because Cowboy hadn't even looked at them as he passed. Still, it was a wonderful sight.

Unfortunately, Cowboy's efforts seemed to be adding a new drift to the fight, and the whole mess was heading toward the mud room. Raven jumped over the broken door on the floor, and hid inside the darkness of the utility room.

Several combatants were struggling in the mud room, before Cowboy finally fought his way in. Once someone stumbled from a punch into the utility room, but Raven merely shoved him back into the fray. As soon as she saw Cowboy's distinctive shirt, she grabbed it and pulled him in, shutting the door on the rest of the fight.

"See if you can get the window open." Raven leaned against the door, trying to hold it shut against the shoves and punches from the other side.

Cowboy fumbled a bit trying to open the window in the normal way, before giving it up. "Painted shut." He looked at Raven. "You okay? That door won't hold much longer."

"I'm fine. For now."

Nodding, Cowboy started searching the floor, and equipment. "Gotta be something here that'll break the window." His gaze fell on the control box. "Maybe this thing'll come loose." He reached for it.

"No!" Raven shouted.

"What?"

Locked in a death grip with Demetri, Dafyd scrambled across the floor. He didn't dare let go, but couldn't get Demetri wrestled into a death hold. Demetri seemed to be experiencing the same difficulty. Dafyd knew whichever one of them won this battle would win it all.

Here and now, in this idiot brawl, everything would be decided between them.

Suddenly he heard a shout.

"Cowboy!"

It sounded like Raven, but who was Cowboy?

Dafyd looked back toward the rear of the house, and

caught of glimpse of Raven in the doorway. If she escaped, he wouldn't have the crimson heir.

As he tried to head to the rear, he noticed that Demetri was doing the same. Yes, they would have the same goal there.

Someone shoved him from behind, and he and Demetri careened into the wall. The battered and splintered wall broke as they hit it, and they fell twisting and turning into the kitchen.

Demetri landed on top of Dafyd, and Dafyd knew he'd lost. Demetri would kill him. Instead, Demetri jumped up, and away, back into the hallway.

Dafyd took a moment to catch his breath. Was Demetri so obsessed with the crimson heir he'd leave an even more dangerous enemy alive?

Shaking himself, Dafyd got to his feet. He stepped back into the hallway, pulling a stake from a large splintered two-by-four as he passed through the opening.

The fight had gone to the rear of the house.

Enough was enough. Now at the fringe of the fight, Dafyd started plowing through by staking one of Demetri's bodyguards, currently fighting Chuck.

Chuck backed away, shocked, then looked up and noticed his rescuer was Dafyd.

"Time to finish this," Dafyd said.

Merely nodding, Chuck leaned against the broken wall, staying out of Dafyd's way. Dafyd grabbed another broken piece of wood that could serve as a stake, and started toward the next of Demetri's men.

He staked the second man, and had restored some sort of order to the hallway, before he stepped into the mud room.

Demetri was throwing himself like a maniac at the closed utility room door. The door was cracking and wouldn't hold long. Four of Dafyd's people were fighting in an odd clump, with one of Demetri's guards, though it would be hard to say who was allied with whom. Two people lay on the floor, but Dafyd couldn't say if they were dead or simply unconscious.

Dafyd chose Demetri as his opponent again, and tackled the man against the utility room door. The door broke, splintering, and they fell through to the utility room floor.

Raven quickly explained about the booby trap, while Cowboy ever more frantically searched for something that would break the window.

Cowboy finally settled on the door for the air conditioner's air filter. His first swing scratched the paint, but did no damage to the window.

The door behind Raven started cracking. Muttering, Cowboy wrapped his shirt around his arm, and grasped the filter door like a shield. A mighty backhanded swing of his contrived shield arm crashed through the glass and wooden crosspieces.

The door started splintering behind Raven, and she knew one more hit would break it. Cowboy cleared the glass shards from the bottom of the window with his shield, and he pulled himself up and out.

As he turned to help her out, Raven jumped away from the door, and a final resounding blow exploded through the door.

Demetri and Dafyd fell struggling onto the floor, striking the backs of Raven's knees and knocking her down. Dafyd, uppermost, had a stake poised to kill Demetri. Demetri reached up grabbing Dafyd's right wrist with his left hand. His right hand, searching for a similar weapon on the floor among the door's splintered remains, grabbed Raven's ankle.

Raven screamed, and kicked out trying to get away. She knew Demetri had unfortunately recognized her cry when his hand tightened on her ankle. She scrambled with frantic urgency toward the window.

Cowboy jumped back up into the window frame, hanging half-in and half-out of the window. He grasped Raven's hand, pulling her to her feet.

Dafyd and Demetri struggled, scrambling, twisting, and revolving on the floor. Dafyd appeared to have the upper hand, but only because Demetri was splitting his attention between the stake in Dafyd's hand and Raven's ankle.

As Cowboy slid backwards out the window, he dragged Raven with him and, because Demetri wouldn't let go, both the skirmishing men.

Raven ended stuck in the window, with her arms and head out, but unable to break Demetri's grip on her ankle. She kicked at him with her free foot, but his hand only clamped down tighter.

Eerily the only sounds outside were her own and Cowboy's heavy breathing. The sounds of the struggle inside didn't penetrate the well-made walls of Dafyd's house.

Cowboy reached around her through the window to grab her under her arms, and he pulled with renewed strength. Raven frantically grabbed at Cowboy's bare shoulders and arms, and kicked with her free foot.

Her foot hit something on the wall, and she inched out the window up to her ribs. The control box. Trying to remember where her foot had hit, she kicked at the same spot with all her might.

Suddenly the house was filled with brilliant, fiery light.

Raven screamed as she felt her legs burn. However, Demetri's hand released her ankle, and Cowboy had her out and away from the window in a flash. Raven could see a dozen burn marks along her jeans, felt pain from the corresponding wounds on her legs. She patted the smoldering spots. Her legs were still functional. She would heal.

The screams of pain and fear from the house were horrible. The smell of burning, roasted flesh wafted out on the breeze. Every window spilled deadly light onto the grass. Raven half expected the grass itself to burn and blaze, but the lawn merely reflected the deep green of well tended turf. Raven couldn't remember when the last time was that she'd seen such color and light. She stared, trembling.

"Sorry about your legs, darlin', but we gotta run." Cowboy grabbed her hand and pulled her down the steps, across the lawn, avoiding the light, and into the blackness of the alley. He kept running, and Raven ran after him. Far into the night.

Light burned his eyes and his flesh, and Demetri found he could no longer hold onto anything, not Raven, not Dafyd's wrist. He shut his eyes and curled himself as much as possible under the howling

Dafyd.

The booby trap, someone had set off Matt's booby trap.

Demetri realized that Dafyd's body had shielded him when Dafyd rolled off writhing and contorting in pain. Instinctively, Demetri reached for the other man, and gritting his teeth against the pain he himself felt, Demetri pulled Dafyd back over him as a shield. Demetri's legs remained exposed, but he used them to propel him toward the window.

As Demetri stood he exposed more of himself to the burning light, and his shield was rapidly shrinking and turning to ashes. He forced himself to release what remained of Dafyd Peack, and pulled himself up into the window. Blessed darkness engulfed his head and hands, and with his last remaining ounce of strength, Demetri pushed himself out the window. He rolled across the porch, away from the death light.

His legs were withered and blackened, and the rest of him burned and raw, but he had survived. Demetri Vasile still survived.

Unable to move himself, Demetri knew he had to get help, or his survival would be only a temporary reprieve. Every breath was pain, but Demetri screamed for Derrick.

Demetri was hoarse, and nearly unconscious when Derrick finally appeared on the back porch.

"Oh man, I thought you were dead," Derrick said, looking him over. "I thought everyone in there was dead."

Yet, here I am screaming my head off, Demetri thought, but he said, "Get me to the van. Get me out of here."

"Right. Right." Derrick looked around as if he hoped to find something to carry Demetri on, rather than actually touch him. "I'll get you back to the hotel."

When Derrick finally did pick him up, Demetri discovered that there was some excruciating pain left that he hadn't experienced. He nearly passed out on the way to the van, and found himself wishing he would.

Derrick laid him on the back seat of the van. "What about the others?"

"All dead. Everyone is dead." Demetri cackled a moment, something between a laugh and a bark of pain. "Dafyd Peack will no longer be a concern of ours."

"Was Khalida Raven in there?" Derrick asked.

"No." Demetri drew an agonizing breath. "She escaped."

"Matt?"

"Everyone else died. Matt, my bodyguards, Dafyd Peack, all of his people, everyone." Frustration and fury allowed Demetri to get it all out. "Now get me out of here."

"Everyone, huh?" Derrick sounded thoughtful, but he headed for the driver's seat.

The pain of driving over LA's rotten streets finally sent Demetri into unconsciousness.

CHAPTER TWENTY-FOUR

Flavian strode through the mansion, feeling decidedly ill. Petra's people had quickly cut the electricity to the mansion, once they'd realized what had happened and how to get to the fuse box. They had already pulled every single one of the abominable light fixtures, and restored the electricity. Flavian almost wished they hadn't, since it merely served to better reveal the carnage.

In the main parlor they found Chuck, huddled under a table, with chairs pulled around to provide some additional protection. He was badly burned and unconscious. He'd been taken away to recuperate elsewhere.

Up in the blue parlor, Sonya, one of Marlynne's assistants had hidden in a table that had a storage compartment. The desperation necessary to induce her to contort herself into that small space made Flavian's heart quake.

Even with the charred and acrid evidence strewn

throughout the mansion, and grouped heartbreakingly around the back door, Flavian feared that he could never completely grasp the horror of those moments.

The only other survivors were in the main security room. Two shocked and traumatized vampires had been trapped in that room for eighty long minutes, watching on the security cameras as their comrades died harrowing deaths unable to do anything other than call for help. The security room had been the only one not rigged with those detestable lights.

Monique had taken charge of the wounded, what few there were, and gotten them away from the mansion as quickly as possible.

The charred remains were impossible to identify by sight alone. The few cases that Flavian knew of where vampires had been exposed to sunlight had all been written off by normal people as cases of spontaneous combustion. He could see now why those cases had left so few clues for the police to decipher.

The bodies had all turned to ash. Here or there he saw a bone, and occasionally a tooth, or a bit of jewelry, but usually nothing remained at all except a human shaped pile of ashes. Clothing and any other flammables had burned with the body.

The walls and floors under the bodies were charred. Other than that and the obvious signs of a brawl in the downstairs hallway, the mansion was unharmed. Cleaning the mansion would take a lot of money and time, and be very hard to explain. However, Flavian knew he had to carry on. He had to continue.

Dafyd had set the organization up that way. It was what Dafyd would have wanted. As Dafyd's chosen successor, it was Flavian's job to keep the organization going.

After forcing himself to search every room, both for survivors and the deceased, even though others had already done so, Flavian left for the office building where Monique had taken the survivors.

He had to know what had happened. They had to know how to prevent this in the future.

Monique met him at the entrance to the Peack's Projects office building, and walked beside him to show him the way to the survivors. "Chuck won't be talking to anyone for a long time, but we think he'll survive. We poured blood down his throat, the purest and freshest we have, but he's still going to be a long time recovering. We think if we keep spooning it into him he'll recover. Sonya can talk, but she's in a lot of pain. We're pushing her to drink a lot also, but again the burns will take time to heal. Tony and Javier would have the most to tell you, they've already been talking with Petra, but," Monique placed a restraining hand on Flavian's arm while continuing to walk, "be careful with them. They're not burned on the outside, but inside they're in a lot of pain."

"I understand." Flavian passed one hand over his eyes, wishing he could forget what he'd seen. "I walked through that entire place. I can't imagine the kind of animals that would do such a thing."

She nodded. "I'm sorting through our whole organization looking for psychiatrists and therapists. This is nasty."

Tony and Javier were in a small conference room with Petra and a few other people from the security team. Eight people sat around the polished wood conference table. Everyone had a glass of blood in front of them, but only Tony's and Javier's had been touched. Flavian was glad that Petra had chosen an atmosphere different from the mansions for this critical interview.

The room grew silent the moment he entered. "Can you bring me up to date?" Flavian asked Petra.

Petra nodded. "Earlier today a team arrived, supposedly from the security installation company to put new lights in the emergency light fixtures. We should never have had those installed."

Flavian stopped her before she could continue. "We'll worry about that later, just tell me what happened."

"Dafyd never contacted me to confirm these changes. He had too much on his mind." Petra held her hand up, probably to acknowledge that Flavian needn't repeat his request to just tell what had happened, so Flavian kept his mouth shut. Petra continued, "Last night Lincoln Daynes brought a woman, a vampire, to the mansion. Dafyd spoke with them, the conversation wasn't recorded, so we don't know what that was about, but the woman returned again tonight. Again the conversation wasn't recorded, but Dafyd locked her in a room upstairs. He didn't request any additional security for her, or give any reason for his actions, so when she broke out, security did nothing to contain her."

Closing his eyes, Flavian nodded and motioned for her to continue. He had no idea what Dafyd was doing in that, and now probably would never know.

"Demetri Vasile arrived, slightly early, but not

significantly so. This was before the woman broke out of her locked room. Demetri and Dafyd conversed in the blue parlor. It was recorded, but there is nothing significant in it. The woman made her way to the rear of the house, to exit, they assumed." Petra waved her hand at Tony and Javier. "Because of the external door cameras, there is no camera in the mud room or the utility room. They expected to hear from Martin who was guarding the back door, indicating whether someone had left the building, but they didn't hear from him. She was pretty, Martin likes all women, and they assumed he was chatting her up. However, shortly after she entered the mud room, Marlynne led one of Demetri's people, Matthew Mann, out the back door for some air. Again Martin didn't report this."

"A double violation." Flavian sighed.

"We know now Martin had been staked. We don't know by whom."

"Had to be the woman," Flavian said.

"Wait until you hear the whole thing." Petra sighed this time. "They called the violation in to Chuck, who was going to check on it, but got trapped behind Demetri leaving the meeting with Dafyd. Since Larry was going to collect Matthew for Demetri, Chuck radioed him about the rest of the problem, and returned to his post."

Petra drummed on the table. "The rest is very confusing. A fight spilled out from the mud room, containing Lincoln Daynes, the mystery vampire woman, and several unknown men, some of whom Tony and Javier recognized as being part of the work crew that installed the new lights. Demetri pushed

Dafyd aside to rush into the fight. Dafyd, his guards, and Demetri's guards followed. The fight destroyed the downstairs hallway, and security received the first call for backup of the night." She turned to Tony and Javier.

In a soft, shaky voice, Tony said, "The strange men made a run for it, and were seen by the rear perimeter guards leaving in a light colored van."

"That sounds familiar," Flavian said.

"Yes, sir. This time we have the entire plate." Tony took a shuddering breath. "After that most of the fight had boiled into the mud room. Shortly thereafter those god-awful lights came on." Tears ran down Tony's face.

"At least four people escaped out the utility room window," Javier said, taking over for Tony. "It had been smashed. The rear perimeter guard saw a man run off just after the van left, in the opposite direction from the van. He couldn't chase the van, but started following the man, until we called everyone back because of the lights. He saw two people running away in the same direction the van took, as he was running back. And he saw Demetri's driver pick someone up off the back porch and leave with them."

"Where was Dafyd?" Flavian asked.

"We don't know." Tony looked up, his voice under control, but tears still streaming down his face. "Dafyd staked two of Demetri's guards, had the fight almost stopped, then he went into the mud room." Tony voice broke, and he closed his eyes.

Flavian looked at Petra. She frowned. "We have to assume Demetri survived. His driver rescued someone.

We can trace Lincoln, and through him, the mystery woman. Perhaps they can clear some of this up. At a guess though, the man running away was in the group that set the trap, and he's the one that set it off."

"Why the delayed timing?" Flavian asked.

"To allow them to get away, perhaps," Petra said. "Fear of being in the building as the vampires died. Or even fear that they'd get hurt also."

Flavian nodded. "Daynes had almost finished his job here for us. Gabrielle was going to talk to him about franchising. We'll have a bit more to discuss, now. We'll put her on that. You concentrate on finding those vampire hunters. We need to teach them a lesson. Me and my people will track down Demetri. And take care of him."

Standing, Flavian turned to Tony and Javier. "You've done well. I'm sorry, so sorry, for what you had to go through. We need you now, still. This organization will carry on. We will continue Dafyd's vision. I promise you that."

Jim walked up to the counter. "I need a ticket please."

The lady behind the counter smiled at him, her uniform all pressed and neat, little wings sewn cleverly over the breast pocket. She smiled at him, gleaming pearly white teeth in nice even rows. He hadn't seen anything like that in along time. She was a pretty woman, a little younger than his mother, perhaps, and a little stout, but she was so normal, and clean, and perky, and stereotypically ordinary.

"Yes, sir. Where did you want to go?"

"Home." Jim had always heard that you couldn't go home again. However, he knew it was vitally important to prove that one wrong this time. "Just home."

Demetri regained consciousness as Derrick gently laid him on the bed in the hotel room.

"Fool! We can't stay here." Just getting the words out hurt Demetri's raspy raw throat. "This will be the first place they'll look."

"Where should we go?" Derrick asked.

"Another city, another hotel. We'll have to hide."

Only as he said it did Demetri realize the problem before him. He had to hide not only from the remnants of Dafyd's organization, who would surely kill him if they found him, but also from his own people. Demetri had filled his organization with hungry, aggressive, opportunistic sharks. He could name at least a dozen that would kill him just to take control.

That didn't even begin to include the number of people in this country, both in and out of his organization, that hated him, and would kill him just for that alone.

Even Derrick might want him dead. That way Derrick couldn't be blamed for what had happened, nor would Derrick be responsible for caring for an invalid. Demetri had to make Derrick think that he had to keep them both alive, not just look out for himself. Demetri tried, but he couldn't even move his arms or legs. He could only barely turn his head.

"We'll need to get a new vehicle." Demetri watched

Derrick's face. He had to sell this one. His life depended on it. "You'll need to rent it with cash, so they can't trace it. I don't know how fast they'll trace the van you have now. We have to leave this city. Immediately. Go someplace you've never been before, because they'll be tracing you through that rental you've got out there."

A variety of emotions and thoughts played across Derrick's face. Fear, frustration, anxiety, fury, resignation each took a turn. Finally, he nodded. As he picked Demetri up he said, "I'll get as much cash as I can. We'll stop at every ATM we pass. I know a place I can rent a vehicle, no questions asked. We'll head for..." he paused. The pause lasted until after he had Demetri settled back in the van.

Demetri struggled not to pass out with the pain. He had to keep Derrick wound up. Keep Derrick from realizing that dumping him would be the fastest and easiest way to escape this mess.

"Nevada," Derrick said finally. "I've never been to Nevada. We'll have to stop somewhere along the way. We'll pick someplace we pass as it gets close to dawn."

"Pick an out of the way, Mom and Pop, roadside tourist trap." Demetri began to relax, it looked like Derrick would keep him around a little longer. "We can feed then, instead of paying."

Derrick grinned back at Demetri, before backing the van out of the parking spot. "Yeah, that'll work." After they'd left the parking garage, Derrick said, "Maybe we should call someone in New York. They could send help."

"Not yet." Demetri winced at the thought of the kind of "help" his people in New York would send. "Most of the ones we need to contact are in the strike team." A blatant lie, but Derrick wouldn't know that. "I have no way to contact them now, part of our security. We'll have to wait at least a few days for them to get back to headquarters before we can contact them."

He saw Derrick's head nod. He'd have to think of another convincing lie later, to keep Derrick from notifying anyone of his crippled condition. Well, once he was able to get around on his own he wouldn't need Derrick any more. Then he'd have to decide if Derrick was worth keeping, or if Derrick would be more trouble than he was worth.

Cowboy ran about two blocks, then stopped at his car.

Raven got in quickly, looking back, but she didn't see anyone following them. As Cowboy pulled away from the curb, she said, "Take me to the club."

"Darlin', that'll be the first place they look for you." Cowboy kept his eyes on the road as he drove, but Raven noticed he checked his mirrors more often than necessary. He too must fear they were being followed.

"I don't think Dafyd told them about me being the crimson heir, or possibly anything else." Raven told him about what had happened to her at the mansion before his arrival.

He returned the favor by telling her how he'd seen the vampire hunters stalking Demetri, and followed them as they followed Demetri back to Dafyd's mansion.

However, he did take her back to the club.

"I'm sorry," he said as he parked in the alley near the stage entrance.

"I know. I'm losing my life here, but it's better than losing my life completely."

"Can I," Cowboy looked longingly at her, "come with you to say good-bye?"

"Sure."

Backstage inside the club was fairly quiet.

"You're late." Manny smiled at her. "I knew you'd be back."

"Your car!" Raven suddenly remembered that she'd left it at the mansion. "Oh my God! Manny, I'm so sorry."

"It was the fellow you were afraid of, wasn't it?" Manny asked.

"Yes, but I forgot your car." Raven couldn't believe she'd done that.

"Don't worry about it." Manny waved this off like it was nothing. "I'll go get it."

"But you don't even know where it is," Raven said.

"No problem. GPS." Manny grinned. "I'll just report it to the police as stolen. They'll find it, and who ever was bothering you will have more problems than they bargained on."

"Raven!" Tina shouted as she ran down the hallway. "Where have you been? We're late!"

Glancing at the clock, Raven realized it wasn't even one in the morning yet.

"Come on, we've got to get onstage," Tina started dragging her toward the stage.

"You don't understand," Raven started.

"No, you don't understand." Clarisa had joined Tina in pulling Raven toward the stage. "There's an agent in the audience and he's waving a contract. He thinks we're back here discussing it. They want us to make a record, immediately. They want us to start touring, the entire U.S., as soon as possible." Clarisa got up in Raven's face. "Now. Big money. Recording contract. Our big break."

Raven glanced back at Lincoln hanging with Manny at the stage door, possibly to keep him away from her good-byes to her friends. She couldn't hear their conversation, and knew they couldn't hear hers. Turning back to Tina and Clarisa, Raven said, "There's something I need to tell you."

"Okay, but make it quick." Tina practically bounced in place with eagerness.

"I'm a vampire." There she'd said it.

"Okay." Clarisa nodded. "So we only work nights, and we only travel nights. Got it." She turned to head to the stage.

Grabbing Clarisa's arm, Raven made her turn around. "No, really. I'm a vampire. You know, fangs and blood and all that."

"Fine. Let's get on stage." Clarisa stepped behind Raven and started pushing Raven toward the stage.

Twisting away from Clarisa and turning to Tina, Raven said, "Would you talk some sense into her?"

Tina grinned at Raven. "We're trying to talk sense into you. We're friends. We accept you as you are. We'll work with it. Now, let's go for it."

Unable to trust what she'd heard, Raven said, "You believe me that I'm a vampire?"

"Oh yes," Clarisa said.

Tina added, "It explains a lot."

"And you don't mind?" Raven asked.

"You going to bite us?" Tina asked.

Raven recoiled. "No, of course not."

"Good, we don't have to hit you," Tina said. "Now let's go make some music. And some money."

"But..." Raven felt overwhelmed. "There's so much you don't know. Like I've got other vampires searching for me."

"While we're recording, we'll go into hiding," Clarisa said.

"Yeah, and when we're on the road, you'll be hiding in plain sight." Tina grinned. "If we're famous enough no one will be able to touch you without half the world screaming for their blood." Her eyebrows wiggled. "Think about that."

"Don't worry about it," Clarisa said. "We're your friends. We'll work it out together."

Stunned, Raven didn't realize they'd coaxed her onto the stage until she heard the crowd roar, scream, clap and stomp behind her. Raven thought about the things she had seen and heard while escaping the mansion. She realized it might be a long time before anyone would be looking for her.

Tina shoved Raven's guitar into her hands. Automatically Raven walked to the mic. Tina sat at her drums. Clarisa picked up her base. All three waved to the audience, causing a crescendo of screaming applause. Tina added a few blown kisses to certain individuals.

Off to the side, Cowboy stood resting one hand on the

stage, shaking his head, but he was smiling while he did it. Though dressed in black, he stood out from the crowd. There just weren't that many Goth cowboys. It was something about his stance, his smile. He should have been wearing a white hat, Raven realized. Good guys wore white hats. She'd have to tell him after the show. Raven sent him a well-what-could-I-do shrug, and found she couldn't stop smiling.

Soaring high on the energy from the audience and supported on the euphoria of friendship, Raven leaned into her mic and shouted, "We are the Sinister Sisters!"

They launched into the first number on the screams of the crowd.

ABOUT THE AUTHOR

D.L. Lawson grew up in the Midwest, not all that far from where nothing happens almost every day. This gave Lawson plenty of time to hone the imagination by reading too many books and watching too many horror movies.

Lawson began writing at the age of twelve and never looked back, except to make sure that no one was creeping up behind and that any noises were all natural in origin.

D.L. Lawson now lives and works in the Southwest, where it's just as spooky as the cornfields of youth, but doesn't snow very much.